CHOICES

Also by Deborah Lynn Jacobs: *POWERS*

CHOICES

DEBORAH LYNN JACOBS

A **DEBORAH** BRODIE BOOK
roaring brook press
new york

Text copyright © 2007 by Deborah Lynn Jacobs

A Deborah Brodie Book
Published by Roaring Brook Press
Roaring Brook Press is a division of Holtzbrinck
Publishing Holdings Limited Partnership
175 Fifth Avenue, New York, NY 10010

www.roaringbrookpress.com

Distributed in Canada by H. B. Fenn and Company, Ltd.

Library of Congress Cataloging-in-Publication Data

Jacobs, Deborah Lynn.
Choices / Deborah Lynn Jacobs. — 1st ed.
p. cm.
"A Deborah Brodie book."
Summary: Overcome with guilt over her brother's death, a teenaged girl shifts
between multiple universes in an attempt to find one in which he is alive.
ISBN-13: 978-1-59643-217-8
ISBN-10: 1-59643-217-9
[1. Space and time—Fiction. 2. Death—Fiction. 3. Grief—Fiction.
4. Identity—Fiction. 5. Brothers and sisters—Fiction.] I. Title.
PZ7.J15213Ch 2007
[Fic]—dc22   2007003439

2 4 6 8 10 9 7 5 3 1

Roaring Brook Press books are available for special promotions and premiums.
For details, contact: Director of Special Markets, Holtzbrinck Publishers.

Book design by Míkael Vilhjálmsson
Printed in the United States of America
First edition September 2007

To Kathryn:
If I had a hundred daughters,
you'd still be my favorite.

Dave and Kathryn, you really came through for me when I asked you to read over the final version of this book and give me your critique within 24 hours! Thanks! (And if you think that's the last time I'll ask for that favor, think again!)

I'm thankful for my Wisconsin critique group, who have become more than crit buddies.

Amy Laundrie, Eva Apelqvist, Donna O'Keefe, Jamie Swenson, Shawn McGuire-Brown, and Sue Berk Koch: thanks for your insightful critiques, for our brainstorming sessions, our coffee dates, our gabfests at the Wisconsin SCBWI yearly retreat, and for being my very dear friends.

It's been a joy to work on another project with Deborah Brodie, my editor, and Steven Chudney, my agent. Thanks to both of you for your enthusiasm and support.

Acknowledgments

...and yet not me'

My hair for one thing

...it of focus

phase shifted, like a double

I wobble ...m, my knees fighting the

...ury shoulder-length

brown hair, eyes normal

way, since one is

Remember.

t? Remember who? And what's

...ts of the mirror.

The dreams are real.

I jolt awake. What a freaky dream,

one where it was me in the mirror and yet *not* me. My hair for one thing, chopped and spiked and dyed deep blue. And my face, my *face*, was out of focus, phase-shifted, like a double exposure with two images badly superimposed.

I wobble to the bathroom, my knees fighting the adrenaline rush that woke me.

I relax when I see my reflection: shoulder-length brown hair, eyes normal—well, normal for me, anyway, since one is brown and the other green—and my face clearly focused.

Then I notice the sticky notes. They rim the mirror in rainbow colors. *Remember. Don't forget him. Read the notebook.*

Remember what? Remember who? And what's this about a notebook?

There's another note, bottom center of the mirror. *The dreams are real.*

Impossible.

I find a notebook on my desk. It's red, spiral-bound, college-ruled. A neon-green sticky note screams: *Read me*.

I open it to see my own handwriting, the back-slanted sprawl of a leftie. I flip through the notebook, noticing the names—Kathleen, Kay, Kate, Kathy.

My memory is fading like an old photograph left too long in the sun. The edges curl and the images grow faint. The colors bleed away, leaving indistinct people with blurry faces.

Maybe that's my mind trying to protect itself. Not for the first time do I wonder if all these lives and time-lines are the products of my own insanity. Kathleen, Kay, Kate, Kathy—how could I have been all of them? And all at the same time?

The people in my dreams? The faces in the mirror?

I'm writing down everything, starting with the party, just as it happened. No, not as it happened. As if it's happening, right now. Who knows? Maybe it is happening, in some other universe.

KATHLEEN

Death Traps

I should learn to drive. I should. Almost eighteen and still I rely on Jen, my best friend, to take me everywhere. But I hate cars. Cars, they're fragile. Tear like tissue paper. Crumple like Styrofoam cups. Death traps, that's what they are.

Those are my thoughts, two hours into a new year. I'm slumped on the stairs that lead to Matt's bedroom, where Jen lies in a drunken stupor. Outside, freezing rain slants down through winter darkness.

Where's my brother, Nick? I called him two hours ago for a lift. What's taking him so long?

"Oops, sorry," shouts a male voice as beer splashes down. A few drops land on my jeans. I look up to see Matt lurch down the smoke-hazed staircase.

"How is she?" I yell over the pounding music.

"Baked," Matt says with a lopsided grin.

I feel like smacking the grin off his face. Jen's baked? Jen never drank, never got high. Until tonight. All it took was Matt, the heartthrob of our senior class. He offers weed, she smokes it. He offers alcohol, she drinks it. It's not that Jen's a pushover. Jen has no difficulty saying no, even to Matt. She just wanted to impress him. Fit into his world.

Some world. Some party. If the music were any louder, my eardrums would explode. My eyes are stinging from secondhand smoke, and I don't mean cigarettes. Countless guys have pressed a drink into my hand. But they can never quite figure out which eye to focus on—the brown one on the left or the green one on the right. They usually settle for staring fixedly at my nose. Like they think I don't notice *that*? After a few seconds of nose-watching, they find excuses to drift away.

I poured the drinks into the dieffenbachia's pot in the front hall. Its leaves are drooping. I guess it can't handle rum and Coke any more than I can.

Matt sways past me on the stairs and looks out the window. I see headlights as a car swings into the driveway.

My brother. *Finally*.

"Uh-oh," Matt says. "The cops."

"What!" I yell.

"Stall them!" He pushes into the throng of people in the living room. He shouts something, but his words are lost in the reverberating music. He switches the noise off and calls out, "Drink it, eat it, or stow it. We've got trouble."

From the living room comes a cacophony of sounds: the clink of liquor bottles; people shuffling around, bumping into each other, swearing and giggling. Kenny, a guy in my English class, stares at the pipe he's holding in his hand as if staring at it might make it magically disappear.

The doorbell rings. Matt motions for me to open it. "Stall," he repeats in a fierce whisper. He runs down the hall, clutching an armload of half-consumed beers, leaving a dribbling trail in his wake.

Stall. Great idea. I should never have let Jen talk me into coming. Yeah, right. That's what I say every time Jen talks me into something. Next time I'll put my foot down.

I say *that* every time, too.

The doorbell rings again. I peek out through the window to see a uniformed policeman, young, skinny, with a prominent Adam's apple. He takes off his cap and mangles it in his hands.

I open the door and slip outside to stand shivering in the porch light. I'm hoping the smell of marijuana hasn't followed me.

"May I help you?" I ask.

"Uh, I'm looking for Kathleen Ker . . . uh . . ." The policeman hesitates, looks at his notes.

"Kerchenko. That's me. I'm she. I mean, I'm Kathleen." I don't understand. Why is he asking for me by name? Uh-oh. He's looking at my eyes. I wonder if I have a contact high. Do your pupils dilate if you have a contact high?

His gaze shifts from my right eye to my left, then drops to his notebook.

"I'm Officer McClaren, Pine Ridge Police," he says. "Your brother's been involved in an accident. Your parents are at the hospital. I'm under instructions to take you there."

"That's impossible," I say. "My brother is coming to pick me up, because Jen pass—" I shut my mouth before I blurt out the rest of the sentence. Because Jen, my ride, is passed out in Matt's bedroom.

"Your brother is Nicholas Kerchenko? License plate . . ." He pauses, flips open a notebook, reads off Nick's license plate number.

What? What's he saying? Nick? In an accident? My head spins as if I've been drinking after all.

"What? How is he? Is he hurt? Is he going to be okay?" I say, tripping over my words.

"Uh, I think it's best if your parents fill you in," the policeman says. "Would you like to get your jacket?"

My jacket is inside the house where people are dashing around, panicking, hiding bottles of vodka and rum.

"No. Let's just go," I say.

He glances at me sideways, but nods.

Cold rain falls. Freezing rain. It slicks the driveway with an invisible but treacherous coating of black ice.

We creep down the road. I'm anxious to see Nick. To make sure he's okay. To hear him laugh and say, "It's nothing, Kath. Just a few bruises. I get banged up worse in a scrimmage."

What if he's seriously injured? Cars, they're death traps. What if he's . . . ?

This drive is taking forever.

I ask the cop, "Shouldn't we put the siren on? And the lights?"

He glances at me and turns his attention back to the road. It takes me a few silent miles to decipher his expression.

It's pity.

Denial

Partway to the hospital, I wonder: had Nadia been in the car with Nick? Then I remember our conversation, when I'd called for a ride.

"Sure, Kath. Where are you?" Nick had asked.

"The address is on the fridge."

There's a pause as he goes to check.

"Okay, got it. Yeah, I know that area. Be right there."

"Will Nadia be mad?" After all, it was New Year's Eve. My parents had gone to Aunt Lydia's, so Nick and Nadia were having a romantic evening alone.

"Nah. She fell asleep at around eleven. I had to wake her up at midnight just to get my kiss." He laughed. "She fell back asleep about two seconds later. I'll leave her a note, just in case."

"Thanks, Nick."

"No problem."

The Emergency Room doors sigh open. I'm directed to a waiting room. On the couch, Mom is sobbing. It's a horrible, ragged sound, like someone is ripping her apart. Nadia, her face streaked with tears, sits beside her, holding her hand.

Dad slumps in a chair to the side of the couch. His elbows rest on his knees, his head down, his face covered by his hands. I think he's crying. More than anything, that shocks me. Oh, God, Nick must really be hurt.

"I tried to call your cell," Nadia says, "but you didn't answer. So I gave the police the address on the fridge." She's talking in a faraway voice, like she's in shock.

I nod. The party was too loud for me to have heard my phone. I sit down on the other side of Mom.

My heart is pounding so hard I think I might faint.

"Where's Nick?" I ask. "Is he okay? What happened?"

Dad composes himself, wipes his face, clears his throat.

"Nick was driving north along State Street," he says. His voice is strangely empty. I get the feeling that if he gives in to his emotions, he won't be able to stop.

"A van was traveling east on Ottawa Drive," Dad continues. "The van had a stop sign. Nick had the right of way. The driver of the van tried to stop but the conditions were too slippery. He went through the intersection and hit Nick's car."

I can hear the sound of the impact. Like the last time I drove, just after I got my learner's permit, and I was stopped at a red light when some idiot plowed into me—*wham*—and the sound of my trunk crumpling was the sound of metal screaming.

Dad's voice breaks. "The van pushed Nick's car across the intersection. It hit a utility pole. They think Nick died on impact."

"He can't be dead." The room sways around me.

"I'm sorry, Kathleen," Dad says. "There was nothing they could do for him."

My vision grays. I put my head down between my knees. It can't be true. I just talked to Nick a few hours ago. Things like this don't happen, they don't.

Out of nowhere, anger takes over. I want to hit something. I jump up, pace around the room.

"What about the driver of the van?" I demand.

"He's fine," Dad says.

"What? Nick dies and the other guy's fine?"

"It was a full-sized van, Kathleen. Nick didn't have a chance." Dad runs his hands through his sparse hair.

"So what's the guy's excuse?" My voice comes out shrill. "Was he drunk?"

"No, not drunk. It was no one's fault."

"No one's fault? You can't be serious. What's his name?"

"Michael Agius. That's what the police told us."

"Some old guy? Some old fart who shouldn't be driving?"

"Young guy," Dad says tiredly.

"Young? Like, what, was he on his cell? Text-messaging with one hand, driving with the other?"

"No, nothing like that. It was an accident." Dad stops my frantic pacing. He puts his arm around my shoulder and leads me back to the couch.

I realize I'm on the edge of hysteria. I fight to calm down. "I need to see him, Dad."

Dad takes a while to answer, as if he's trying to find the right words.

"They don't recommend that," he finally says. "Nick was trapped in the car, between the pole and the van. They had to call for the Jaws of Life."

His voice breaks again. He turns away, and I know he's crying.

I should break down. I should cry, shouldn't I? Isn't that what people do? But, for some reason, I can't. All I can think is: it can't be true. Nick can't be dead.

Refusal

It's freezing outside. An Alberta Clipper, they call it. A cold air mass moves down from Canada, turning Wisconsin into a giant ice cube.

Why didn't the cold come a day earlier? Twelve hours earlier? Turn the freezing rain to dry, powdery snow, like the stuff that is sifting down outside. I watch it from where I'm sitting on the living room couch. It's beautiful, nothing but a harmless white dusting on the road.

I didn't sleep last night. Every time I closed my eyes I heard the sickening crunch of metal, loud, so *loud*, echoing in my head. Was that the last sound Nick heard before he died? Did he suffer?

I just want to go back. Go back to where I let Jen talk me into going to the party. Go back, and this time *say no*.

I remember the conversation I had with Jen, word for word. We were sitting on my bed, listening to music, eating popcorn.

"Why can't we have a sleepover at my house?" I had suggested. "We'll have a movie marathon."

"That's what we always do, Kath," Jen said.

"So? What's wrong with that?" I said, grabbing a handful of popcorn.

Jen pulled her fingers through her dark hair. Expertly, she fashioned it into a French braid, going by feel alone.

I finger-combed my own shoulder-length hair, wondering if I should cut it shorter. "I don't know. If my parents ever found out that Matt's parents will be out of town, they'd kill me."

"Don't tell them that part." Jen pulled her hair back out of the braid, twisted it into a sloppy bun.

"I don't know . . ."

"Kath, come on. Live a little."

"I live," I said, feeling defensive.

"On the sidelines," said Jen. "Like when we went to Six Flags."

"Well, someone had to capture the moment," I said. "I was your official cameraman."

"You didn't go on a single ride."

"But I got some great video."

"And the time we went to the water park?"

"Those slides can be dangerous," I argued. "You enter the water so fast you can lose your bikini top."

"And when have you ever worn a bikini?"

"Well, never," I said. "So, obviously, I've never lost my top."

Jen snorted. "Look, just come to the party, okay?"

"Why? Because it's *Matt's* party?"

"What's wrong with that?"

"What do you see in him anyway?"

"He's hot," she said, as if that explained everything.

"He's an immature *boy*," I said, "whose acne just cleared up last year."

"Kath, you set your sights too high. Who are you saving yourself for?"

"Something better than Matt."

"Look," she said, "it's one party. One night. Just come with me."

"Why don't you ask Maya?"

"She has to babysit her little brother," she said.

Poor Maya. If her parents said Maya had to babysit, then Maya had to babysit.

"What about Steph?"

"Family vacation down south. You're my only hope, Kath. You have to come. I can't go alone, now can I?" Jen blinked rapidly, letting her long bangs tangle in her eyelashes.

So I went to the party. And because of me, Nick is dead. It's all my fault.

Or is it? What about Jen? Pushing me to go. Guilting me into it.

And then she'd gotten loaded. She knew I couldn't drive home. What kind of a friend abandons you like that?

If she had stayed sober, I wouldn't have needed to call Nick. He'd still be alive.

The doorbell rings, cutting through my thoughts, breaking the dust-thick silence in the house. Trojan, our Great Dane, answers from Nick's room, a querulous woof, as if to ask, "Isn't anyone getting that?" Mom is in the kitchen, making another call in a long series of calls.

"Yes, closed casket. The funeral is Sunday." That's my mother's voice, almost a whisper. It breaks when she gets to "funeral."

From my position on the living room couch, I watch Jen as she stabs the bell again. She steps back, peers through the front window, waves at me.

I ignore her. Refuse to make eye contact. *Go. Just go.*

She taps on the window. She's standing in the flower bed, holding up the jacket and purse I left behind at the party.

I shake my head. She's the last person I want to talk to right now.

"I'm sorry," she shouts. Coming through double-paned windows, it's muffled but clear enough that I get it.

I don't budge. *Sorry* doesn't quite cut it.

Her face goes blotchy the way it always does when she's trying not to cry. She hangs my purse and jacket on the doorknob. She slouches down the driveway, feet dragging, head dropped low.

My throat closes up. What am I doing? We've been friends since middle school. How can I let her walk away, hurt and angry? She might never talk to me again. I know Jen. She's not the forgiving type.

I should call her back, I should. I can imagine myself doing it. I'll fling open the door and call her name. She'll race back up the drive and launch herself through the door. She'll throw her arms around me and nothing will have changed between us.

But then I hear that sound again, in my head. Metal twisting. Crushing. Screaming. I look out the window and watch Jen drive away, leaving whirls of powdery snow in her wake.

Grief

Neighbors trickle over. They bear loaves: lemon, blueberry, zucchini, carrot. Mom double-wraps each loaf in aluminum foil. Labels each one: Zucchini Loaf, Mark and Sylvia Anderson; Blueberry Loaf, The Petersons; Lemon Loaf, from Leslie next door. She lays them in the freezer, side by side, like little metallic coffins.

Aunt Lydia arrives. She envelops me in a hug, big-boned and pillow-soft. "How're you holding up, honey?" Her voice, roughened by thirty years of cigarettes, grates in my ear. It's oddly reassuring.

"Okay," I lie.

"Where's your dad?" she asks.

"In the den. Watching sports. He only comes out to eat," I say.

"We all grieve in our own way," Aunt Lydia says. Just the same, her lips purse in disapproval.

Aunt Lydia heads to the kitchen, bearing gifts: cabbage rolls, pierogi, poppy-seed cake. For after the funeral, she says.

We all grieve in our own way. I've thought of going in there, of offering whatever comfort I can. But the truth is this: the only person who could comfort my father is gone.

The Stranger

I run my hand over the coffin, and feel the perfect smoothness of polished wood. I refuse to believe Nick is in there. He's alive. In some time and place, he *must* be alive.

I'm still in denial, I know it, I do. I should have worked through this stage. Denial, anger, what's next? I don't remember. I'm stuck.

People arrive for the visitation: first a dribble, then a flood. Dad is the manager of the Pine Ridge Hardware Store. Mom works at the public library. Between the two of them, they know practically everyone in town.

Dad sits in a far corner, as distanced from the coffin as possible. His face is gray and flat, like an image embossed on a coin. Mom sits stiffly upright, ghostly calm.

"So sorry for your loss, Emma," people say to my mother. "You never think your child will go ahead of you."

"How very tragic. It's a mercy he didn't suffer."

"He's in a better place now."

If they notice me at all, it is to say to Mom, "Thank goodness you still have a daughter."

Or, "Kathleen must be a great comfort to you."

No one asks me how I feel. No one seems to realize that I've lost a brother.

Maya and Steph arrive. "So sorry," they murmur. They give me awkward hugs, and soon leave.

Jen is conspicuously absent. This hurts. But I was the one who refused to talk to her yesterday, when she returned my things. I deserve this, I do.

But can I forgive her? I can't answer that.

The room stifles me. The air is gone, replaced by the reek of too many flowers. Mom is retelling the death story for the hundredth time. I hear phrases like "broke his neck" and "Jaws of Life." I'm two seconds from losing it.

Anger. Stage two. If I ever met this Michael guy, this guy who killed my brother, I'd kill him. Slowly. Painfully.

I push through the crowd and break out into the hallway. There's a bench against one wall. I put my head between my knees, fighting dizziness.

A blast of cold air hits me. It smells like fresh snow and suede. Someone sits beside me, says in a quiet voice, "Are you okay?"

I look up into the deepest, darkest eyes I've ever seen. Large, set in a wide, tanned face.

My reflex is to say, "I'm fine," but my body takes over and I dissolve. The stranger puts an arm around me. I turn into the comfort of his shoulder and drip tears onto the soft suede of his jacket.

I come to my senses and pull away. I don't know what to say, I don't. It's like we are in the same space, but that's impossible. I don't even know his name. I've just blubbered all over a stranger. I should be embarrassed, but I'm not. It's like we are already connected; we just don't know it yet.

The stranger pulls an old-fashioned handkerchief from his pocket. I notice his hands, large and square with short fingers. He blots away the tears on my face. This reminds me of Nick, of the time I fell off my bike, right into an enormous mud puddle. Dirty water ran down my face and my clothes. Nick had taken the edge of his T-shirt and used it to wipe the mud off my face.

The memory sets off a fresh wave of grief.

"You're Nick's sister?" the stranger asks.

I nod, not trusting my voice.

"I'm sorry," he says.

I'm about to blow my nose, but the ick factor of snotting into a handkerchief stops me. I snuffle instead. The sound is loud and rude, but he doesn't seem to notice.

"It hits you at unexpected times," he goes on. "You're going along and keeping it together and all of a sudden it hits you just as hard as the first time."

I nod again.

"I lost my parents when I was sixteen," he explains. "Mostly I don't think about them much, but then something will remind me—like the smell of marinara sauce bubbling away on the stove—and it hits me. Like hearing the news all over again. It's like they've just died. Each and every time."

Fresh tears run down my face. I taste salt at the back of my throat.

"How do you go on?"

"You just do," he says. "You don't have a choice."

I look into his eyes, so dark, nearly black.

"We haven't met, have we?" I ask. "Do I know you?"

"No." His eyes smile. "Not yet. I'm Luke."

"Kathleen," I say. "Did you know Nick well?"

"Not really," says Luke. "I study culinary arts at the college. I was in the Student Union, and I ran into Nick. Literally. I had a full cup of coffee and turned around without looking, and there he was."

"You spilled your coffee all over him?" I ask.

"He was really nice about it," Luke says.

"Yeah, that was Nick," I say.

"We had coffee together a few times after that. Our schedules seemed to coincide, so we'd show up needing caffeine at the same time." There's a pause, and then Luke stands up. "I'd better go."

"Do you want to go in there first?" I ask, motioning to the viewing room.

"No. I just moved to town a few months ago. I won't know anyone," he says. "I just wanted to tell someone how sorry I am."

"People keep saying that," I say, "but you're the first person I actually believe."

I hand him back the handkerchief. He stuffs it in a pocket and walks toward the door. Then he stops. I swear he hesitates for five seconds, while I hold my breath. He turns, comes back to sit beside me.

"Look," he says, "I know how hard it can get, in the days and weeks after. Let me give you my number. If you need to talk . . ." His voice trails off into uncertainty.

I fish a scrap of paper and a pen from my purse. Luke writes his name and number down in a bold hand. I tuck the paper into my purse. Luke absent-mindedly pockets my pen.

"So, uh, if there's anything I can do . . ." he says.

And then something strange happens. It's like his face shifts out of phase. It's like watching a cheap movie, where the image never quite focuses. I could swear the air shimmers around him, just a little, like the way a road shimmers on a hot summer day. I rub my eyes and the illusion disappears.

He walks to the door, glances back, and gives a slight wave before he leaves. That's when I realize something. The whole time we'd been talking, he'd looked me straight in the eyes. Both eyes. Not the brown one and then back to the green one and then back to the brown one.

I feel as if, for the first time, someone has actually seen me.

Double Exposure

It's the second night of visitation. I'm again sitting on the bench in the hallway. People arrive, whispering their "sorrys." I'd hoped Luke might come again, had scanned the crowd looking for his dark hair and suede jacket. At one point, I was sure I caught a glimpse of him at the back of the room. By the time

I'd pushed through the crowds of people, he was gone. Or, maybe it wasn't him after all.

Jen doesn't bother to come. Again.

I can hardly blame her. I'd rejected her, not the other way around. Still, she could have made allowances. She could have put herself in my shoes. She could have called, or shown up tonight, if not for me, then out of respect for Nick.

Just as I'm thinking this, the front door opens and in walks Jen. She rushes over to hug me. Snowflakes shine like tiny stars in her dark hair. They melt, leaving sparkly beads of moisture.

"I'm sorry," she says. "I tried to get out of work early but the bastards wouldn't let me go. How're you doing, Katydid?"

I brush the tears away. She hasn't called me Katydid in ages. My anger dissolves.

"Oh, Jen, I'm so glad you're here," I say. "Last night, when you didn't show up, all I could think was—"

"What do you mean?" She pulls back and looks at me like I've lost my mind. "I told you ahead of time that I couldn't come. I had to work late, remember?"

"What?" I say. "When did you tell me that?"

"When I came over. When I brought your purse and your jacket." Jen does her nervous thing, twisting her hair in her hands. "Are you sure you're okay, Katydid?"

"Not really." The world swirls around me and goes

gray. When it clears, she is there with a glass of cold water. I gulp it down and then choke. She pounds my back. It doesn't help. When I stop coughing, she says, "You *do* remember me coming over, don't you?"

"It's all a little fuzzy," I say.

"It's the shock," Jen says with her usual air of authority. "It does that to you. Post-traumatic stress disorder. I bet that's it. Are you having trouble sleeping? Eating?"

"Yes. And yes," I say.

"But you do believe me, don't you?" she asks. "I did have to work yesterday."

"Yes, I believe you," I say, shakily. At this point, I don't know what I believe.

"Look, let me take you home," she says. "I'll go in and pay my respects and stuff, and let your parents know you're leaving."

"Okay," I say, content to let her decide for me. My brain feels like congealed oatmeal. The thoughts travel only so far and then bog down.

Jen drives me home. Fat snowflakes drift down from a softly clouded night.

"I'll come in with you," she says when we arrive at my house. "I'll make warm milk with pepper in it. It'll help you sleep."

"That's disgusting," I say.

"Ooooh, a spark of life," she says. "Hot chocolate then? With marshmallows?"

"No, thanks, Jen. I need to go to bed." That's a lie, but I need time to think this out alone.

She gives me an understanding hug. "Okay. See you tomorrow."

Once inside, I turn on all the lights. I fill the kettle with water, but my hand is shaking so much it takes me three tries to plug it in.

What's happening to me? I seem to have two sets of memories superimposed on each other. I remember Jen ringing my doorbell. She stood in the flower bed, the snow swirling at her feet. I remember thinking that Nick's death was her fault. But then I'd thought: *how can I let her walk away? She might never talk to me again. She's not the forgiving kind.* I had thought about opening the door and calling her back. But I hadn't. I had let her drive away.

But there's the other memory. I'd forgotten it, until Jen reminded me. Now it comes back to me, in all its clarity.

I had run to the door. Yanked it open. Shouted, "Jen!"

She wheeled around, dashed up the driveway, slipped once, dropped my jacket and my purse, then grabbed me in a fierce hug. Her cheek, pressed against mine, was cold and wet with tears.

"I'm sorry, I'm sorry," she said. "It's all my fault."

Those words melted the anger in me. I'd been wrong to blame her. She hadn't forced me to go to that party. I'd gone of my own free will.

We sat down on the couch and I held her hand so hard it must have hurt, but she didn't flinch. Tears coursed down her face, like the tears that flowed down mine. We stayed that way until Aunt Lydia brought us hot chocolate and homemade chocolate chip cookies.

It has to be a true memory. It has to. I remember the marshmallows, three of them, melting into the creamy hot chocolate. I remember the way the cookies were warm from the oven, so that the chocolate chips were sticky. I remember saying to Jen, "I'm sorry I left you at the party. Did I get you in trouble?"

And I remember her reply. "No, I told my parents I stayed over at your house. I told them I didn't call because I didn't want to wake them."

I remember thinking her breath smelled like chocolate and wondering if mine did as well.

The kettle whistles, breaking up my thoughts. In the dead silent house, it sounds like a scream.

What's happening to me? Which memory is true?

I choose a ginseng tea bag and pour boiling water over it. Ginseng is good for the memory, I think. Or is that ginger tea? I can't remember.

Maybe Jen is right. It's the shock. Post-traumatic stress disorder. You think you remember things one way, but you don't. I must have called Jen back. That's the only explanation.

Routine. Stick to routine. That's what you're supposed to do when the world crumbles around you. Routine gets you through.

I brush my teeth, wash my face. My eyes resemble poached eggs. I go into my parents' bathroom and find Mom's night cream, the one that is supposed to reduce puffiness.

I'm so tired that my face phase-shifts in the mirror, a double exposure with images that don't quite match. For a moment, I feel disoriented, like my world has changed in ways I can't begin to comprehend.

Of course my world has changed. Of course I can't make sense of it.

Tomorrow we bury Nick.

After

The limo takes us home from the cemetery. Jen follows in her car. I wish she was with me, here in the limo. My parents seem turned to stone, not talking, their eyes blank.

I try to be like them, to not think, not move. But I can still hear my mother's weeping at the gravesite. Can see the flowers on the casket, obscenely alive.

Can feel where the rose pierced my finger with a thorn. The rose I placed on Nick's casket when I said good-bye.

People are already at the house when we arrive. Relatives, friends, and neighbors gather in small groups, drinking beer and wine and whiskey with soda. They nibble on appetizers, little pork kebabs and chicken fingers, stuffed mushrooms and meatballs. They talk and they laugh, as if this is a party. Aunt Lydia orchestrates. My parents are robots, speaking when someone speaks to them, mostly saying "thank you" and "I'm so glad you could come."

It's like when Nick died, he took part of them with him.

Jen saves me. She loads up plates of food and leads the way to my bedroom.

"Eat," she orders, thrusting a plate of food at me. She takes a bite and talks around it. "Hey, this is good. What is it?"

"City chicken," I say.

"Doesn't taste like chicken," she comments.

"It's not. It's chunks of veal and pork, coated with bread crumbs, then fried, and then baked."

"Then why's it called city chicken?" she asks.

I'm too tired to answer. The greasy smell of the meat turns my stomach. I set down my plate and walk through the bathroom that connects my room to Nick's. Trojan, asleep on Nick's bed, opens his eyes, sighs, and closes them again. I breathe in deeply to smell the trace of Nick's cologne in the air. There's a fainter underlying scent of the foot spray Nick used each day. He has notoriously stinky feet.

Had, I correct myself. Past tense. *Had*.

I can't believe he's gone. It feels like he's still here, in all the bits and pieces that made up his life. Here's a photo of Nick right after he scored a winning touchdown this fall. He's streaked with dirt and sweat and looks insanely happy. Here's another of him and Nadia, taken last Christmas. He's laughing. I can almost hear it in my mind, a joyful, unrestrained laugh. His walls are covered with pennants from colleges across the states. I can almost see him standing on the bed, lining up another pennant and securing it with pushpins.

"Just ten more states to go, Kath," he'd said a few days before he'd died.

Ten more states. Ten empty places, waiting on the wall.

"It feels like he could just walk in that door," Jen says, coming into the room.

I nod. "Sometimes, I think I see movement or hear a noise in here. I could swear he's back."

"That's normal when someone dies," she says. "It's your mind playing tricks on you."

"Well, in my case, it's just Trojan," I say. "He won't leave Nick's bed. It's like he's waiting."

Jen sets down the plate of food and rubs Trojan's ears. He groans a long note of contentment.

"So how about you, old boy?" she asks. "Are *you* going to eat?" She puts the emphasis on "you" and gives me a stern look.

"Only if you hand-feed him," I say, answering for Trojan.

"Poor baby," says Jen. "Want some country chicken? *Someone's* got to eat it."

I'm about to correct her—it's *city* chicken—but it seems unimportant.

She pulls a bit of meat off the skewer and holds it in front of Trojan's nose. He opens one eye and lazily takes her offering. Once he swallows it, he snaps to full wakefulness and sits up, sphinx-like. His eyes swivel from the meat to Jen's face and back to the meat.

She laughs and feeds him one morsel after another. Once the city chicken is gone, she pulls apart chicken wings and offers him shreds of meat.

"Does he like cabbage rolls?" she asks.

"I don't know."

Jen sets down the plate with cabbage rolls and pierogi. Trojan eats the sour-cream-smothered pierogi first, one bite for each piece, then daintily strips the cabbage leaves off the cabbage rolls. He devours the beef-and-rice filling in seconds.

"See," says Jen. "At least *he* has the sense to keep his strength up."

"Okay. I give up," I say. "Go get me some chrustyky."

"Oooh, good idea," says Jen. "C'mon, let's put on a movie in your room. You can't stay here staring at Nick's stuff all night. Trojan, you too."

She gently tugs on Trojan's collar. Trojan trots through the bathroom and leaps up onto my bed. I follow him and hear Jen shut Nick's door with a firm click.

By the time I have the movie started, Jen has returned with the largest plate of chrustyky I've ever seen, along with two giant glasses of milk.

Jen grins. "I stole the whole platter when your aunt wasn't looking."

The deep-fried pastry melts on my tongue and fills my mouth with powdered sugar. It's the first thing I've eaten in days. It tastes like heaven.

"Oh," says Jen, popping a pastry into her mouth. "I forgot to tell you. Something weird happened just as you were pulling away in the limo. I was walking to my car. Everyone else was gone. This guy walks across the cemetery, like he'd been waiting. You know, like hiding behind some big monument."

"Uh, huh," I say, to keep her talking. My breathing speeds up. Who would show up at the end when everyone was gone? Maybe someone who didn't want to intrude? Someone like Luke?

"Anyway," Jen goes on, "this guy goes up to the

casket and takes a flower out of the pile and tucks it into his jacket."

"Are you sure he wasn't placing a flower *on* the coffin?" I ask.

"No, he definitely took it *off* the coffin. I just thought it was strange, was all," Jen says.

"Uh, Jen, was he on the short side? Stocky? Dark hair and a brown suede jacket?"

"Yeah, brown jacket," Jen says. "Do you know him?"

"He showed up at the visitation, the first night. He knew Nick from college."

Jen answers with a loud sniff. "Sounds like a weirdo to me."

"No, actually he wasn't," I say. "He was really nice. I felt, I don't know, kind of a connection with him."

"Well, I think any guy who skulks around grave-yards is creepy," Jen says. "And then to steal a flower from a gravesite—"

I cut her off. "Maybe he wanted a memento. You know, something to remember Nick by."

"Creepy," Jen repeats. "Stay away from him."

I'm tempted to comment about Jen's skill at judging character. Matt's character, for example. But I do the smart thing and keep my opinion to myself.

Jen climbs on top of the bed with me but leaves enough room for Trojan to slide between us. I pretend to watch the movie, but my attention is elsewhere.

I'm thinking of Luke, of how he let me cry all over him and how gently he wiped away my tears.

Flying Monkeys

"Kathleen? Are you getting up? Should I call the school and tell them you won't be in today?"

"Huh?" I rub the sleep out of my eyes. Mom hovers over my bed, still in her pajamas.

"Where's Jen?" I peer through the bathroom into Nick's room. Trojan has his head on Nick's pillow, his feet hanging over the side of the bed.

"Jen?" Mom sounds puzzled. "She hasn't been here since the accident."

"What? She stayed over last night."

"Oh, sweetheart, maybe you *should* stay home." She places her hand on my forehead. "What happened between you and Jen? Want to talk about it?"

"Nothing happened. She was here last night," I insist.

Mom frowns. "Maybe you should talk to the doctor, honey. I'm not going to work today. I'll drive you in."

The doctor? But I'm not sick. Just . . . just what? Imagining things?

"No. I'm fine. Really." I head for the shower. "I must have dreamed it."

Mom doesn't look convinced as she leaves,

closing my bedroom door behind her. I stand in the bathroom and look into Nick's room. Trojan has woken up. He shifts position to lie with his face nestled between his front paws, his expression melancholy. Gone are the plates of chicken bones, left after Jen had stripped the meat off the wings. Gone are the bamboo sticks that held the city chicken. Gone is the plate with the cabbage leaves, left after Trojan ate the filling in the cabbage rolls.

I go back to my room and pop open the disk drive on my TV. There should be a movie there, the one we watched last night.

It's not there. What's going on? My heart beats rapidly and the room feels stiflingly hot. I throw open my window and take great gulps of January air. Outside looks normal, a half moon shining down on crusty snow, a faint sunrise glowing on the horizon.

Does a person who's gone crazy know they are crazy? Or does everything seem ordinary to them? Oh, look, a flying monkey. How nice.

Wait. Insanity doesn't run in my family. Or does it? Wasn't there a cousin who ended up in a psychiatric hospital? Multiple personalities or something?

Trojan shivers and makes a rumbling sound deep in his throat. I go back into Nick's room. Trojan groans as I run my hand between his big, bony shoulders. He sighs and licks my chin. *Hold on to this*, I think. Trojan is real. Not an illusion or a delusion or whatever crazy people get.

Did Jen sleep over? Or did it happen the other way I remember it? I remember going to the funeral with my parents. Maya and Steph were there, along with a few other people from school. I went to the cemetery in the limo, then came home with my parents. People came over, filling our house with noise. I had wanted to escape to my room, but Aunt Lydia said, "You'll feel better if you keep busy." I'd brought out trays of food and made sure everyone had a drink.

I had felt so utterly alone.

And now it all comes flooding back. My anger at Jen. She should have come to the funeral. She should have. After years of friendship, she owed me that much. Sure I'd turned her away, but I'd been angry. She could have tried to understand. But no, not Jen. She holds grudges; nurses them like babies.

So, fine. Be that way. See if I ever speak to *her* again.

I glance back at my room. It had been a dream, my memory of Jen staying over. It had to be. There was no other logical explanation.

Midnight Marauder

"You're going like that?"

"It's only a few blocks, honey," Mom says. She's

wearing her pajamas under her winter jacket. I hunch down in the passenger seat, hoping she doesn't get into an accident. Wouldn't that be fun?

When I get to my locker, I find Jen is at hers, only two down from mine. She doesn't say hello; doesn't even look my way. I watch her key in her combination, then step back as books avalanche down. It's the usual routine.

I pick up her Chemistry book and hand it to her. I'm waiting for her to say something. *I'm sorry* would work for me. But she gives me a hurt look, with tears in her eyes, as if I've wronged *her*. As if I should apologize first. She's the one who didn't have the decency to come to the funeral, and she wants *me* to apologize?

I walk away without saying a word.

By lunchtime, I'm ready to go home. If one more teacher asks how I am holding up, I might just tell them the truth. I'm not holding up, thank you. Not at all.

I arrive at the cafeteria to find Jen already at our table with Steph and Maya. They're talking, but they fall silent as I approach. Maya gives me a sympathetic look but doesn't invite me to join them. I walk past, heading for a table in the leper section, near the restrooms. I slump into a chair and open my Biology text. The words swim on the page like sluggish amoebas.

"Mind if I sit down?" comes a voice.

"Huh?" Sunny, the school freak, wants to sit with me? I glance around, wondering who put her up to it.

"Of course, if you don't want to be seen with me . . ." she says, moving away.

"No. Please," I motion to the chair across the table. She sits down. I try not to stare at her two-inch-high jet-black hair. It's tipped in silver, to match her eye makeup and fingernail polish.

"Sucks, doesn't it?" She runs her finger over the multiple rings in her left eyebrow. "My male parental unit died last year."

"I'm sorry," I say reflexively.

"Why? You didn't kill him. Cancer did." She shrugs and plays with the line of studs that rims her ear.

"People have three stock phrases," Sunny continues. "I'm sorry for your loss. I heard the bad news. How are you holding up?" She pulls a plastic container out of a paper lunch bag. "Aren't you eating?"

"Not very hungry."

She shoves the container over and hands me a spoon. "Try this. Tabbouleh."

The grains taste nutty, with a hint of lemon and mint. "Not bad," I say.

"I can't stand the stuff. My mom's a vegetarian. Do me a favor? Eat that so I don't have to throw it out. I'm getting a burger." She grins at me, showing dimples on either side of her mouth. The smile transforms her face, making her seem almost normal.

She hands me her paper bag and heads for the à la carte counter. She's in a black top and a short black skirt. Above knee-high boots, her legs are encased in silver fishnet hose, matching her tipped hair. If nothing else, she's color-coordinated.

Inside the paper bag I find round, flat cookies. They taste like oats and butter. Along with that is a small bag of cashews and a container of apple slices, sprinkled with lemon, sugar, and cinnamon.

I surprise myself by polishing everything off by the time Sunny returns.

"Whoa. You ate that crap?" Her expression is one of mock horror.

"I haven't been eating much lately," I confide.

"Sudden death. Kills the appetite," she says, totally serious.

I don't know whether to laugh or cry. I settle for a question. "What does Sunny stand for?"

"Sunshine. My mother is a leftover from the seventies. Fits my disposition, doesn't it?"

I don't know what to say. I've only seen her smile once. Then again, maybe I've never really noticed her before, except to think of her as weird. I glance over at Jen's table. Even from here I catch the look on Jen's face, a mix of disbelief and disgust. She shakes her head, as if to say, "What are you thinking?"

My face gets hot. Who is she to judge? She abandoned me when I needed her the most. Screw her, then. And Maya and Steph? They are clearly in Jen's camp. Screw them, too.

I suffer a bus ride home surrounded by freshman and sophomores. My parents and I have our first dinner alone since Nick's death. I try to pretend Nick is missing dinner because of a late class, but his chair is *empty* in a way that it had never been before. We pick at tuna casserole (Tuna Casserole: Mrs. Gibson, three doors down), followed by zucchini loaf (Zucchini Loaf: Mark and Sylvia Anderson).

The only sound is the clinking of silverware against our dinner plates. It makes me realize how Nick had always carried the conversation, entertaining us with stories about his professors or football practice. He had an inexhaustible arsenal of jokes, not all of them polite.

"Oh, Nick, really," Mom always said in response to an off-color joke, but she had always laughed along with the rest of us.

I try to think of a joke but my mind is blank. "How was work?" I ask Dad, instead.

"Huh? Oh. Busy. January sale. Ran out of cordless drills," Dad says.

"Will you order more?" Could I ask a more lame question?

"I guess," says Dad, shrugging. He eats mechanically. I doubt he tastes the food, which is probably a blessing, considering the gluey quality of the casserole.

"How was your day?" I ask Mom.

"Quiet," she says, sipping her iced tea. She's still in her pajamas. Her hair sticks up in random clumps. I wonder if she has showered.

I give up on conversation. I try a bite of tuna casserole, but my throat closes up. I'm choking on the sorrow in this room.

"Would you load the dishwasher?" Mom asks. She wanders off into the living room and settles on the couch with an old photo album. Baby pictures of Nick. His first steps. The day Dad took the training wheels off his bike.

Dad clears the table, then heads for the den. A moment later, I hear a sports channel blaring.

I fill Trojan's bowl with kibble, then add the tuna casserole from my plate.

"Dinner, Trojan," I call out.

A quiet groan from the vicinity of Nick's room is my only answer. I go in to find Trojan on the bed, exactly where I left him this morning.

"Come on, you big, old horse," I grunt, tugging on his collar. "Dinner is served."

Reluctantly he leaves Nick's room. He wolfs down his food, laps up his water, slobbers dog spit all over the floor, then pads back to resume his vigil.

"You're welcome," I mutter, wiping up dog drool.

I escape to my room. I try to do homework, but all I can think about is this: *did he suffer?* Did he feel the impact? Did he feel his neck break? His leg shatter? Did he know he was dying? Or did it just happen— *wham*—painless? One second here, the next second *gone*?

And the guy who hit him. That Michael guy. Where is he now? Living a normal life? Coming home after work, cracking a beer, sitting down to dinner. Lounging in front of the TV. Living. What gives him the right? He should be paralyzed, *his* neck broken, unable to move. *That* would be justice.

The phone rings, jarring me out of my thoughts. I wait four rings, then the answering machine picks up. I hear a voice from the grave. "Hey, you've reached the Kerchenkos. You know what to do."

I hear the beep of the machine, and then, very quietly, someone say, "Oh, *shit.*"

I recognize that voice. I run to the phone. "Nadia? Is that you?"

"Hi, Kath," she says in a choked voice. "I'm sorry. I wasn't ready for that. His voice. For just a second there, I thought . . ."

"I know. I'll change the message."

"No, don't. Not for me, anyway. Look, I was wondering, could I come over?"

That sets me back. Nadia and Nick started dating in high school. When Nadia chose to live at home and go to college in Eau Claire, half an hour away, Nick made the same decision. They had planned to marry once they finished school.

"Since when do you need an invitation?" I say.

"Thanks, Kath."

The doorbell rings ten minutes later. She's huddled on the porch, arms wrapped around herself as if for warmth.

I wonder why she rang the bell. She hasn't done that in ages. But Nick is dead and the funeral is over. She must wonder if she still belongs here.

I let her in, and she breaks down sobbing.

"Oh, Kath, I miss him so much."

I don't know what to do. Part of me wants to hug her and tell her it's okay, that I miss him too. But another part of me, the part I don't like very much, wonders why she is coming to me. Doesn't anyone get it? I miss him too.

In the end I give her an awkward half hug. Still sniffling, she heads for the living room.

"Hi, Mom," she says, sitting down beside my mother. For some reason, that bugs me. It shouldn't. She's been using that name for years. But today it bugs me.

"Want to join us?" Nadia offers.

"No thanks," I reply. "I have tons of homework."

"Okay," says Nadia. She glances down at the photo album, open on Mom's lap. "Oh, I remember that one. The Northwoods camping trip."

I leave them to reminisce, and wander into Nick's room. I open his closet and run my hands over his clothes. They smell like fabric softener.

Grief hits me without warning. Like Luke said. It's like I'm hearing the news for the first time. I hold my hands over my mouth to muffle my sobs. My whole body shakes with the force of them. Nick's not coming back. I try to remember his face and the sound of his voice, but I can't.

I cry until my chest hurts. When I go into the bathroom, thinking to run cold water over my face, I see something that sets off a fresh wave of sadness. It's a toothpaste tube, scrunched in the middle. It drove me crazy when Nick mangled the tube like that. I'd have to smooth it out before squeezing it from the bottom, the proper way.

Well, I won't have to worry anymore, will I? I squeeze the toothpaste around until I get the kink out of the tube. Why did I get mad at Nick for this? It's so petty.

Trojan whines from Nick's room, a high-pitched keening that sets my nerves on edge.

"What?" I say. "Am I supposed to be a comfort to you, too?"

Trojan raises his head, grumbles in a low, complaining voice.

"He's gone. Okay? He's not coming back. Get over it."

Trojan turns his eyes away from mine and sighs heavily.

Great. I'm taking out my anger on a dog. How mature.

"Trojan, I'm sorry. Want to go outside?"

Trojan throws me a sullen look. Clearly, he holds a grudge as well as Jen. I get his lead from the closet by the front door. As I do, I pass by the living room. Nadia has left. Mom's gone to bed. The zucchini loaf from dinner sits open on the coffee table. It's only half eaten, so I close up the foil so it won't dry out. When I pass by the den, I see Dad slumped over in the easy chair, snoring. Should I wake him up? Make him go to bed? I settle for covering him with a blanket.

Trojan is still on Nick's bed when I return. I clip the lead onto his collar, but he isn't in a mood to cooperate. I tug gently. Trojan throws me a look of annoyance, then inches off the bed, stretches, yawns, and trots toward the back door. He gives me this look, like, "Well, coming or not?"

That's a Great Dane for you. They'll do anything you want, but they'll make it look like it was their idea all along.

Trojan drags me through the snow, suddenly eager to pee. I look away, out of some perverse need to respect his privacy, while Trojan lets loose a steaming yellow stream onto Mom's lilac bush.

Then he stops in midstream, leg still lifted. The fur between his shoulder blades bunches up. He woofs, deep in his throat. He strains at the lead, pulling me toward the front of the house.

It's overcast, but I can see a car parked at the curb. I hold Trojan back and watch as someone roots around in our recycling bin. Dad put it out after dinner, for the early-morning pickup.

Trojan lets out one sharp bark. The person grabs something from the bin—a plastic bottle?—and hops into his car. It's a dark color, small and boxy. I think it might be a Mini. He takes off so fast that he nearly skids out.

Trojan growls, as if to say, "And don't come back, either."

"Yeah, you said it, boy." I rub his ears and he quiets.

I watch the retreating taillights with a growing sense of unease. Who is going through our garbage? And more important, why?

Predator?

"Honey, you're going to be late for school."

"Whaaa . . .?" I check my alarm. I must have forgotten to set it.

"Are you decent?"

"Yeah."

Mom opens the door. She's wearing black pants and a gray sweater. Her makeup is perfect.

"You're going back to work?" I ask.

"Going back? I went back yesterday. Don't you remember?"

Yesterday? I have a distinct memory of her driving me to school in her pajamas and winter jacket. I remember how embarrassed I'd been that she hadn't bothered to put on clothes. What if we'd had an accident? What if one of the teachers had come up to the car to convey his or her sympathy just as I was getting out? What would I say? Oh, pardon my mom, she's grieving in her own way? In her jammies, in broad daylight, in the car.

"Honey, what's wrong?" Mom asks. "Are you sick?"

Nope, nope. Not sick. Crazy. Nutty-crackers. Certifiable. Ready for the nice people in their pretty white coats to come and take me away. I'm strait-jacket material, I am. Loony bin, here I come. Prepare the padded cell. Get out the *good* drugs. The ones that make you forget.

Mom's giving me a funny look. I have to pull it together, *fast.*

"I'm fine, Mom," I say. "Can you drive me in this morning?"

Mom glances at her watch. "Jen will be here in about ten minutes. It makes me late when I drive you in."

Jen? Ten minutes? But she wouldn't give me the time of day yesterday. That's why I'd eaten lunch with Sunny. Hadn't I?

"Okay. I'll hurry." Though for what, I don't know. Jen won't be coming.

I hop into the shower. I'm throwing on clothes when I hear the front door open.

"Hey, Kath. You ready to go?"

There she is, my old friend, standing in the front hall.

"Jen," I say stupidly. "You're here."

"Well, duh. Like every other day. Hurry up. I don't want to be late." She grabs my coat from the front closet and tosses it at me. She peers into the living room. "Oooh, is that cake?"

"Uh, yeah." I grab the zucchini loaf off the coffee table. I hand it to Jen, who opens it and exclaims, "Oooh, lemon loaf. My favorite!"

Lemon? No, it has to be zucchini. I remember last night, when I closed up the foil so the loaf wouldn't dry out. It was zucchini, not lemon.

My stomach flip-flops. My brain aches, as if it has swollen too big for my skull.

I add *stark raving mad*, *barmy*, and *delusional* to my list. Clearly, I am not in my right mind. Whose mind I'm in is totally up for discussion.

Jen drives, managing to shift gears, turn corners, talk, and eat lemon loaf simultaneously. She's the same old Jen I've always known: dark brown hair, red cheeks, thick lashes that keep tangling with her bangs. Nothing has changed.

Nothing and everything. Again, I have two sets of memories, one sharper than the other. I remember eating lunch with Sunny yesterday and taking the bus home. I remember how angry I had been that Jen hadn't come to Nick's funeral. Nadia came over and spent the evening looking over old photos with Mom and eating *zucchini* loaf. Some guy had rifled through our recycling bin and taken something out.

But on top of that is a different set of memories. I ate lunch with Jen and Maya and Steph yesterday. I didn't actually eat, but I managed to drink a soda and nibble on some chips. Jen drove me home after school. And that night, when Nadia came to visit, I gave her a big hug. She had gone into the living room, to look over old photos with Mom. After a moment of hesitation, I'd joined them. We'd eaten lemon loaf.

So which set of memories is true? How can you tell if a memory is real, anyway?

Jen swings into a parking spot. She brushes crumbs off her coat as she gets out of the car. She holds up the foil-wrapped remains of the lemon loaf. "Can I keep the rest?"

I nod. We walk side-by-side through the icy parking lot.

"Jen, if you were going crazy, would you know you were going crazy? Or would you just go crazy?" I ask.

"Nah, I don't think crazy people know they're nuts," she answers. "There's that loony guy who hangs out on Main Street. You've seen him, right? Skinny guy, about fifty? He walks down the street arguing with an invisible companion. Waves his fist at the guy, yells, calls him names. I think he actually sees the guy, like he's right there."

"So he doesn't know he's lost his mind?"

"Maybe he hasn't. Maybe he really *does* have an invisible friend. Maybe he's in an altered state of reality. Maybe he's talking to a ghost. Maybe we're the crazy ones, because we can't see them."

I shudder. "I wish you hadn't said that."

"Oh, Kath, you haven't seen your brother's ghost, have you?"

"No. Nothing like that. It's just that I've been forgetting things lately. Or I remember them differently from how they happened."

"You just lost Nick. It's normal to have scrambled brains for a while, to get distracted and forget stuff. Or maybe you have early Alzheimer's."

"That's what I love about you, Jen. Always the optimist."

"Good thing you keep me around then." She throws an arm around my shoulder and marches me to school. She smells like lemons.

I zombie through the rest of the day. At lunchtime, I join Jen at our table, along with Maya and Steph. They talk about the usual: the latest reality show that Maya's parents won't let her watch, which colleges have sent acceptance letters, who will probably be valedictorian this year, who is going with whom to the Senior Prom.

I don't join in. None of it matters, anyway. Jen notices I'm not eating and gives me half her peanut butter and jam sandwich. I take a tiny bite, chew, swallow mechanically, but the peanut butter sticks in my throat. I feel disconnected, like I'm watching from a distance. Are these really my friends? Is this my life? Or should I be over there, in the leper section, sharing lunch with Sunny?

Finally the day ends. Jen and I are heading out the door when she says, "Whoops. I left my English book in my locker. Here, you go warm up the car."

I take the key from her, but I have no intention of starting her car. I'm juggling my books and my purse while trying to take off my gloves so that I can open the passenger door. The cold stiffens my fingers almost immediately. I drop the key. When I bend down to grab it, my books skitter out of my arms. As I'm picking them up, I slip on the ice and fall on my backside.

There I am, sitting on the ice of the parking lot, my books, Jen's key, my gloves, my purse all scattered, and my rear end hurting. It's suddenly too much. I won't cry, *I won't*, but then I break down.

"Here, let me help you," says a quiet voice.

It's Luke. He gathers up my things and pulls me to my feet. "Rough day?"

I sniff back tears, making an unladylike sound. "You were right. You're going along just fine and then it hits you—*wham*—just like the first time you heard the news."

He puts his arm around my shoulder and gives it a slight squeeze. I'm sure he means it as a brotherly gesture, but it makes my heart go *kaboom*. He smells like suede and cologne. I don't want him to take his arm away, but he does.

"It gets better," he says.

"But it's not," I say. "It's getting worse. I'm so mixed up. I feel like I'm going crazy."

"It's started," he says.

That's such an odd thing to say. I search his face for clues. The phase-shift thing happens again, just for a split second. It's like seeing a double exposure. I shake my head and his face appears normal.

I'm about to ask, "What's started?" but Jen arrives. She grabs her car key from my hand, opens the door, says, "Let's go." She gives me a nudge, not quite a push but close enough. I can't believe how rude she's being. I set my feet a bit wider and resist her efforts to get me into the car.

"Jen," I say in a pointedly polite voice, "I'd like you to meet a friend of Nick's. This is Luke."

"Hi, Jen," says Luke, giving her a warm smile.

Jen isn't impressed. She folds her arms and says, "So, what brings you back to high school, Luke? A little old to be lurking around, aren't you?"

Luke's skin isn't quite dark enough to hide the flush that colors his cheeks.

"I'm not so old that I can't remember when school lets out," he answers. "I wanted to make sure Kathleen was okay."

"She's fine," Jen says curtly. She jerks open the driver's door and slides in. The car starts with a roar. "Get in, Kath."

I'm so embarrassed I could die.

"It's okay," Luke says. "I'll catch you later."

He walks away as I get into the car.

"What was that all about?" I demand.

"He's *the one*," she says, almost hissing. "The skulker. The one who stole a rose off Nick's grave."

"He was Nick's *friend*, Jen," I say.

Jen looks over her shoulder to back up. "So *he* says. Did Nick ever mention him?"

"No, but there were lots of guys at the funeral that Nick never mentioned."

Jen grinds the gears putting the car into first. She joins the lineup of cars leaving the parking lot and taps her fingers on the steering wheel.

"Look, you don't know anything about this guy. He could be a predator. I mean, why is he hanging around? He's, like, twice your age."

"He's not twice my age," I say.

"Ha," she says. "You told me he was a college student."

"*We'll* be college students next year," I argue.

Jen pulls forward as the line moves ahead. "He's creepy and a predator and he's stalking you."

"And you watch too many slasher movies." I look out the window to see Luke walking across the parking lot. What he does next makes my breath freeze. He opens the door of a black Mini and gets in. I can't be sure, but it looks an awful lot like the car I'd seen last night.

I mean, not *last night* last night. Not the night I ate lemon loaf with Nadia. The *other* last night. The one where I'd gone to my room and let Nadia and Mom peer over old photos and eat zucchini loaf.

Which *last night* was real? I can't tell.

If you were going crazy, would you know?

Brother Substitute?

I am awake and I am afraid. Will Jen come to pick me up, or is she not speaking to me? Will Mom go to work, or will she throw her coat over her jammies and drive me to school? Will Sunny offer me a vegetarian delight for lunch, or will I be eating with my old friends—Jen, Maya, Steph?

I want to burrow under my blankets and stay there. I can't get Jen's suspicions out of my mind. Is Luke a predator, as she claims? Would a predator hold you while you cried? Show up at school just to see if you were okay? And what about that connection I'd felt? That sense of trust, of being safe and protected?

Or was I looking for a brother substitute? But the feelings I had when he put his arm around me—those weren't the feelings you have for a brother.

My head aches. Too much thinking. Time to get up. Face the day, whoever's day it is.

After going through the motions of showering, drying my hair, and brushing my teeth, I head to the kitchen. My stomach is churning with what I hope is hunger but fear is anxiety. I make toast, slather it with jam, and take a big bite.

Nope, not hunger. This is definitely anxiety. I toss the toast in the garbage, then realize I should have given it to Trojan. I fish it out, but there are coffee grounds mired in the jam. Trojan loses out.

There's no sign of Dad, which means he's left for work. I find Mom in the living room, slouched on the couch in her bathrobe. An open library book is in her lap, but she isn't reading it. She's sipping a large mug of coffee. I sit beside her and say, "How're you doing?"

She says, "Fine."

But she isn't fine. There's a bottle of brandy on the end table.

I can't believe it. My mother, the iced tea drinker who has maybe three drinks *a year*? We all grieve in our own way, Aunt Lydia had said. But my mother, putting brandy in her morning coffee? I feel like I've stepped into a different world. No, a different *universe*.

"Are you going to work?" As soon as I say the words, I realize how stupid that sounds.

"No, honey. I'm not quite ready. I need to take a few days off, just to collect myself."

She doesn't slur her words, but there's something careful about the way she speaks. Like she's afraid of slurring. She is deceptively calm, but I know a storm is raging just out of sight.

"So, I guess I'll get ready for school," I say.

Mom squints at her watch. "Better hurry. Bus will be here soon."

Okay. Looks like I'm eating with Sunny today. I shower, then grab my jeans and pink cashmere sweater. I check my image in the mirror. Sunny and I will look ridiculous sitting together. I rummage though my closet and find nothing. I go into Nick's room and find camouflage pants in his closet. He used to go paintballing in them. They smell like fabric softener, spring breeze or summer sunshine or something.

I pull them on, adjust the drawstring, and fix the length with safety pins. Next, I throw on Nick's football jersey. It comes down to my knees and feels like a hug.

I am barely in time for the bus.

Gym Socks

Of course Jen ignores me. What did I expect? It hurts, but not as much as before. I realize I'm actually looking forward to eating lunch with Sunny. When I arrive at the cafeteria, she's sitting with a guy I don't know. She sees me, waves me over. I notice she has changed the tips of her hair to neon green. The color matches her nails.

"Kath, this is Weed," Sunny says.

"Weed?" I've seen him around school but didn't know his name.

"Yeah. It's a moniker and a calling card, all in one. The teachers insist on Jonathan Riley Dawson, my given name." Weed's eyes are bloodshot and I suspect he's been dipping into his own wares. His face sports more hardware than Dad's store. He drawls his words, like he has all the time in the world. But he has a certain rough cuteness about him. I think it comes from his shaggy brown hair and almost-girly gray eyes.

I decide I like him, even if he is baked. He pulls

something out of his knapsack. A pair of white socks?

"Here's the socks you loaned me for gym class," he says, slipping them into my purse.

"B-but, I . . ." I stammer.

"Freebie," he says. "Gotta go." He unfolds his gangly body and leaves.

"Did he just give me what I think he just gave me?" I ask Sunny.

"Gym socks," Sunny says, giving me a wide-eyed innocent look. "You don't have to use them. Throw them out if they don't fit."

"Do you, uh, wear gym socks?" I ask.

"Sometimes. When I'm in the zone."

"Which zone?"

"The creative zone. When I paint. Hey, why not come over tonight?"

"Should I bring my socks?" I grin at her and she grins back.

"Nah. I have lots." She passes over her lunch bag. "Eat this for me, okay?"

As she gets herself a burger, I pull the items out. Peanut butter and green sprouts on brown bread that looks homemade. A container holds granola, with oats, nuts, raisins, and cinnamon. A small Thermos contains vanilla yogurt. The fruit today is dried apricots.

I wolf it down in record time, wondering why I

seem to be able to eat only what Sunny gives me. Maybe because it doesn't come with a side order of guilt.

Letting Go

My mother is asleep when I arrive home from school. My father orders a pizza, and we sit down to watch a college football game. Dad doesn't talk to me.

He hasn't said anything to me, to accuse me or blame me for Nick's death, not even once, but just the same I sense his disappointment. I'm not Nick, his football-playing, sports-nut son. I'm me, the person who hates sports with a passion. I bet if Dad could have Nick back but had to let me go, he'd do it. Oh, he'd be sad about losing me, to be sure. Dad loves me, in his own way. It's just that he loved Nick more. If it came down to a choice between us, I'd lose.

I've taken only a few bites of pizza, but I can't eat any more. I give the rest of my slice to Trojan and tell Dad I'm going to Sunny's house. He nods and grunts, without taking his eyes off the TV.

I escape out the front door. The air, fed by a fierce west wind, feels like liquid ice. I wish I'd worn a hat or scarf, but I am face-naked and ear-vulnerable. I walk backward, counting the blocks to Sunny's house.

Sunny opens the door. She looks different, dressed

in brown pajama bottoms and a matching top. Her bare feet are adorned with three—no, five—toe rings. Each toenail sports a different color, but all are shockingly vibrant.

She takes me by the hand and draws me into the house. I barely have time to kick off my boots. She pulls me along a hallway that's painted pizza-sauce red. Tea-light candles, held in brass wall mounts, throw flickering shadows.

I feel like I'm moving into another dimension.

The house opens up at the back. I think it might be an addition, larger than the original house. To the right is a kitchen. The counters are gray marble, the appliances stainless steel. Then I look to my left and forget about the kitchen.

It's a studio. Sunken, two steps down, pine floors and walls, floor-to-ceiling windows on two sides, skylights in the ceiling. This place must hum with natural sunlight during the day.

Paintings adorn one wall. They vary in size from eight by eleven inches to maybe three by five feet. I walk up to the nearest one. Purple base, swirls of brown, orange, and yellow, accents of white and gray.

"*This* is what you paint?" My mouth hangs open, like Trojan's when he's eyeballing his dinner bowl.

Sunny shrugs. She smiles in a self-effacing way.

"Sunny, this is like . . . uh, who did that painting with all the swirly stars?"

"Van Gogh," she says. "*Starry Night.*"

"Yeah," I say. "Like that. Only better. Wilder. You're a genius!"

"Nah. I just paint what I feel." She leads me over to a black leather couch and a coffee table that holds a grouping of white pillar candles. Sunny lights them and goes into the kitchen. I take off my coat, but there isn't anywhere to put it, so I settle for dropping it on the floor.

Sunny returns with steaming mugs of tea and a plate of brownies.

"You might get hungry," she says, lighting up a pipe. I can tell by the smell it is definitely *not* tobacco. My stomach churns. The smell takes me back to the night Nick died.

"Sunny, could you not do that?" I ask.

"Why?"

"I hate the smell."

"What do you mean? Here, just try it."

"No thank you." I get up to leave.

"C'mon, don't be so rigid."

"I'm not rigid. Besides, what will your mother say? Where is she, anyway?"

"Yoga class. We'll burn incense. She'll never know."

This is insane. I don't belong here. But where do I belong? I'm certainly not Jen's friend.

Maybe Sunny's right. I'm too cautious. I'm afraid

to try new things. Just this once wouldn't hurt. Besides, look at Sunny. She's not a pothead. Look at those magnificent paintings that she's created. She just uses the stuff to relax a little. Maybe I *am* too rigid. It would be nice to let go, just this once.

The smoke burns the back of my throat as I inhale.

Blue Midnight

Trojan, snoring with his head on my chest, wakes me up. I try to remember last night and dredge up a memory of walking home through a sky that swam with stars. Everything felt a little softer around the edges, as if the world had blurred. Halfway home, I had the feeling I was being watched. I wheeled around, hoping to catch someone in the act, but overbalanced and fell in the snow. That set me off into a fit of giggles.

My laughter stopped at my front door. Would Mom or Dad recognize the smell on my clothing? Would they take a good look at my eyes?

I needn't have worried. Mom was snoring on the couch, still in her bathrobe, an empty glass and a half-full bottle of vodka beside her. I covered her with a blanket. Dad had gone to bed. Trojan came out of Nick's room and whined at the door. He seemed desperate. Hadn't anyone taken him out?

I clipped on his lead and took him for a pee. He was so funny, really, the way he lifted one leg. That set me off into helpless laughter again. Once inside, I filled his dog bowl. He ate ravenously, then followed me back to my room and jumped up on my bed.

That sobered me immediately. He'd stopped waiting. Did he even remember Nick?

I'd fallen asleep to the sound of Trojan's breathing. He woke me a few times in the night, when he shifted position, but I'd fallen back asleep quickly.

And now it's a new day. Trojan groans and I push him off me. I walk into the bathroom and grab my toothbrush. I glance at my reflection in the mirror, wondering if my eyes are bloodshot.

Oh, no. I've really done it. I could swear I told Sunny no, that cutting and dying my hair was definitely *not* a good idea. I must have smoked more than I thought. I sit down on the toilet, trying to remember. Yes, I'd talked her out of it. It wasn't *me*, I'd said. But she'd argued that change is good, and after Nick's death I needed to do something wild and different to get out of my rut. She'd taken the scissors and methodically hacked off my hair, leaving a three-inch stubble. Then, using Blue Midnight hair color, she'd given me a "whole new outlook on life."

My mother is going to kill me. Maybe I can wear a hat until it grows in. Or maybe it's a temporary dye, the kind that washes out in a few weeks. Oh, *please*, let it be temporary.

I scrub my hair three times with clarifying shampoo, but when I get out of the shower it's still deep blue. I blow-dry it and it sticks up all over in choppy spikes. It looks like someone gave me a haircut with a weed-whacker.

Fine, then. If it wants to stick up, so be it. I grab some gel from Nick's room and apply it with a vengeance. No sense in going halfway.

Now my problem is what to wear. I'll look like a blue-haired idiot in my usual conservative clothes. So I pull on Nick's camouflage pants for the second day in a row. I pair them with an orange T-shirt that Nick got when he walked Trojan in the Paws for Charity Walkathon last year. Over that, I throw Nick's paintball jacket, camouflage green, beige, and gray.

I look like a goth army cadet.

Dad has left for work and Mom is still snoring on the couch. I lock the door behind me as I leave. As I walk out to the road, the bus breezes by. I shout and wave, but it doesn't stop.

Great. Just great. A north wind whistles through my spiked hair, freezing the gel and turning my scalp into a greasy ice ball. I'm wearing a coat over Nick's jacket, but the wind finds its way in. My hands, in thin gloves, are so frozen that I can't flex them. My backpack weighs a ton and is getting heavier with every step.

I'm about to admit defeat and trudge home. I hear a car behind me. I move over to let it pass. But it pulls alongside me and slows to match my stride. It's a black Mini.

"Cold?" Luke asks.

"I'm fine."

"Could I offer you a ride?"

I'm thinking of what Jen said. He's a predator. "No, thanks."

"I know what you're thinking. Never get into a car with a stranger."

"That's right."

"I didn't offer you candy," he says. "That makes me safe, right?"

"You have a point there," I say. Besides, why should I worry about what Jen would think? Isn't it about time I decided for myself? But I'm pretty sure he's the same person who took a water bottle out of my recycling bin. What's with that?

"It's nice and warm in here," Luke says in a cajoling voice.

"Look, I need to know something first," I say. "Did you take a water bottle out of my recycling bin?"

He looks startled, and then laughs. "You're joking, right?"

"No. A few nights ago some guy was fishing around in my recycling bin. I was outside with Trojan and—"

"Trojan?" His face shows his amusement.

"My dog. Long story. Anyway, this guy drove a small car that looked like a Mini."

"Well, they did make more than just one Mini," Luke says. "C'mon, Kathleen. Let me drive you to school."

A predator, Jen had said. Stalking you. But I look at him, at his dark eyes and that lower lip that sticks out more than the upper. He doesn't look like a predator. He's just watching out for me. Trust yourself, Kathleen, I'm thinking. Do what you want to do, not what someone else tells you to do.

I stop walking. The car stops. I get in.

What's Starting?

I hold my hands gratefully over the heater and try to rub them back to life. Luke notices and reaches over to turn the heater to full. In the small confines of the car, his arm brushes against me. It's nothing, but my breathing speeds up just the same.

"Better now?" he asks.

"Much."

"I like your hair."

"No you don't."

"Yes, I do. It reminds me of my green period." He says it with a perfectly straight face.

"Green?"

"Bright green," he says, grinning.

"Why'd you dye it green?"

"Well, my rainbow hair was getting too many strange looks," he says.

I laugh, trying to imagine him with rainbow hair. "How long ago was this?"

"Oh, a while ago. Before I had to act like a responsible adult."

Ouch, that hurts. He thinks of me as a kid. I wonder how old he is, anyway. Certainly not twice my age, like Jen said. But definitely older. Twenty-one? Twenty-two?

"So, what's the story about your dog's name?" he asks.

"It's really not that interesting," I say, still annoyed by his "responsible adult" remark.

"Ah, c'mon," he coaxes. "Is he really named after a box of—"

"No," I say, cutting him off.

We arrive at school.

"Would you like me to pick you up after?" Luke asks.

"No thank you," I say in a cool tone. "I'm quite capable of taking care of myself."

He flushes. "I've offended you. About your dog."

"No, of course not." I start to open the door but he reaches out and touches my arm.

"Don't be angry. Please?" He rubs his finger along his lower lip, looking both sexy and miserable.

My anger scales down a notch. He thinks I'm angry about the dog remark? If I tell him I'm mad about the "responsible adult" thing, he'll *really* think I'm a kid.

"It's okay," I say, maybe a little grudgingly. "I'm just a little touchy lately."

He leans toward me. "Listen, you have every right. You have to give yourself time."

His tone is so earnest that my eyes burn. I'm going to cry in about two seconds, I know it.

"Hey, none of that." He reaches into the glove compartment and pulls out a clean hanky.

"Do you always have those around?" I ask.

"Pretty much. My grandparents raised me, after my parents died. Grandma gave me dozens of these." He glances at his watch. "Whoa, you're going to be late for school."

"Who cares? Why don't I skip out?"

"No." He reaches across me to open my door. Freezing air rushes in.

"Have a good day," he says.

I don't move.

"Go." He gives me a little push.

My feelings flip again. I'm tired of everyone telling me what to do. And I don't like being treated like a kid.

"Fine. Good-bye," I snap at him. "Thanks for the ride."

"You're welcome," he says as I stomp away. The

wind catches his words and rips them apart. It's only as I cram my coat into my locker and then rush to class that I realize something. I forgot to ask him what he meant the other day, when he showed up after school.

It's starting.

For Every Action

In my first class, Ms. Frye does roll call. When she calls my name, I put up my hand. She gives an audible gasp. Her hand flies to her mouth as if to block her words. For the entire class, she doesn't call on me or look at me. It's like I don't exist.

Of course, the rest of the class is staring, with mixed reactions. Surprise is the most predominant. I can almost see what people are thinking: that's not like Kathleen.

Mr. Groshek, in second hour, is at least half-cool about it. He glances at me as I walk in and does a double take. His hand drifts up to pat his own balding head.

"Quite the change," he says, but his look is sympathetic.

Ms. Kramer glares at me in third hour. She makes me feel like I'm contagious. Yeah, like everyone will cut their hair and dye it deep blue just because I did. Way to be paranoid.

At lunchtime, I'm greeted by whispering and people turning around to check me out. I guess the news traveled. I saunter past my old table as if I don't care what they think. Steph's jaw drops down. Jen sticks her nose up in the air and snorts. Maya gives me an uncertain half smile, like I'm wearing a pumpkin on my head instead of spikes.

Sunny grins at me like we share a great secret.

"Hey, girlfriend. How do you like your new look?"

"Uh, Sunny, how many pipes did we, uh, I mean, how many times did we change our socks last night?"

She pushes her bag lunch across to me. "Lost count. Did you get home okay? You didn't get lost or anything, did you?"

"No, I was okay. A little light-headed, maybe."

"Yeah. Clean socks do that to you," Sunny says. "Wait till I get some of the good stuff."

"I'll pass." The paper bag makes a crinkling noise as I open it. Peanut butter and honey on dark brown bread, a banana, a small bag of cashews, and an orange. There's a plastic knife, which puzzles me at first. Then I look at the banana and clue in. The knife slides through the banana with a satisfying smoothness. In a few seconds I have a peanut butter, honey, and banana sandwich. I sprinkle the cashews on for good measure and bite in.

It's heavenly. I swear if Sunny wasn't feeding me, I'd have starved by now.

"Where's Weed?" I ask, once I come up for air.

"Got suspended. They found gym socks in his locker."

"Oh. That's too bad." I peel the orange and cram an entire slice into my mouth. Juice runs down my chin and I swipe my hand across it.

"Don't worry." Sunny stuffs half a burrito into her mouth, chews, and swallows. "Our supply is safe."

"Hey, no. I didn't mean that. I mean, I'm sorry about the suspension."

Sunny throws back her head and laughs. She has even, white teeth. No fillings. "You're so serious, Kate. Lighten up."

Kate? I'm Kate now? I chew my way through sticky peanut butter, smooth honey, and sweet banana.

Kate. Yeah, that works for me.

KATE

An Equal and Opposite Reaction

Mom's awake when I arrive home. She's at the stove, stirring something in a pan. On the counter I see a box of instant dinner. Just add chicken, it says. How gourmet.

I go up behind her and give her a hug. She's still in her old terry robe. How many days has she worn it? It gives off a sour smell. Or maybe that's Mom.

She turns around. "Oh, my goodness. Kathleen. What happened to your hair?"

She uses a tone of voice like I've just nailed a kitten to a barn door. "It's just hair, Mom," I say.

"Just hair? Your hair was so beautiful. Now look at it. How could you do this to me? So soon after . . ."

Do this to her? I didn't do anything to her. It's hair dye, that's all. What's the big deal? And what does she mean, so soon after Nick died? When am I supposed to dye my hair? A year after?

Besides, look at her. Great role model she is.

"I'm going to my room to do homework." I lock my door and throw myself down on the bed. I crack open the *Canterbury Tales*, but I keep reading the same page over and over. The front door squeaks open, then shuts. Dad's home. I hear him talking to Mom, hear her voice going shrill. There's a knock on my door.

I open it, then sit down on my bed. "Go ahead. Your turn."

"Don't you think this is a little irresponsible?" Dad asks. "Your mother doesn't need this right now."

I'm about to say something like, "I don't need this shit either," but I know my father would go ballistic if I spoke to him like that.

"I'm sorry," I say. "I didn't do it to upset her. She's not doing so great since . . . since Nick . . . uh . . ."

I can't say the word. *Died*. I can think it, but I can't say it aloud.

"Give her a little time, Kathleen," Dad says. "She'll pull things together. Why don't you come help her with dinner?"

Time. That's what Luke had said, too. Give yourself a little time.

So I go back to the kitchen. "Need some help?" I ask Mom.

"You can make a salad," she says.

I feel her eyes on me the whole time I'm washing

lettuce and chopping vegetables. Finally, I say, "I'm sorry."

"That's okay," she says with a trace of a smile. "It'll grow back."

And the thing is this: I'm not so sure I *want* to grow it back.

KATHLEEN

Splitting

I wake up in my bed, tangled in my covers. Something tickles my cheek and I jump, thinking it's a spider. But it's only a strand of hair.

A strand of hair? Oh, no. My hands shake as I reach up to touch my head. No spikes. Just soft, shoulder-length hair.

I struggle to free myself from the comforter. I need to see myself in the mirror. I have the awful thought that I'm in the Twilight Zone. Maybe I'll have a pig face. Maybe no features at all.

But I'm normal. I run my fingers over my eyes, still mismatched, and my hair, brown, and my nose, turned up at the end. Ski slope, Nick used to say. He'd run his finger down my nose and pretend to be a skier launched into the air.

Multiple personalities. That has to be it. I'm two people, Kathleen and Kate. One does things the other would never do. I bet I'll split again, like that old movie *Sybil*. Seventeen people in one body. Gets a little crowded, but you can manage, right? Give everyone a chance to be in charge. Let the responsible personalities clean up the mistakes of the wild ones. Sure, a body-by-committee.

No, no. That makes no sense. If you have a split personality, you have no memory of what the other person did. And your hair doesn't change and then go back to normal.

Unless you are crazy. Psychotic. Like that cousin no one talks about, the one who was hospitalized. Maybe I only *thought* I was Kate. Only *thought* I'd cut and dyed my hair. Looked in the mirror and *saw* spiky blue hair. Walked to school and *thought* I talked to Luke. Thought he gave me a ride. And all the time, I was like the crazy man in town, talking to a companion who doesn't exist.

What's real? What's not? I can't tell anymore.

It's started. Is that what Luke meant? A slow slide into madness? Or is it a quick descent?

There's a knock on my door. "Come in."

It's Mom, dressed for work. "Better hurry, hon. Jen will be here soon."

Good. That grounds me a little. Let's see: Mom's sober, she's going to work, Jen's driving me in. Okay. I can handle this. I can go to school and pretend to be sane.

I should call Luke, I should. Do I still have his number? I'd stuffed it into my purse.

My hands shake so hard that it takes me a few tries to open the zipper on my purse, then a few more tries to unzip the inner pocket where I'd put the slip of paper.

It's not there. Frantic, I dump the contents of my purse onto my bed. I find one wallet, two pens, a hairbrush, three mints, cherry-flavored lip balm, and a paper clip.

But no slip of paper. Of course not. Why would it be there? Just because I remember putting it there? Ha, ha. Get real.

I *am* crazy.

Not So Much

It's strange how a crazy person can still act normal. I get through the entire day at school, doing the usual things, without any problems. I remember being Kate yesterday. I remember Mom being upset about my hair and Dad telling me to give her time.

But I also remember being Kathleen. I had gone to school as usual. Jen had come over after dinner. We'd done homework, then watched a movie. Nadia had come over and played gin rummy with Mom. Dad had, as usual, retreated to his den and his TV.

It makes my head ache just to think about it. I feel like I'm standing in quicksand and sinking fast.

Jen drives me home after school. Nadia's car is in our drive. I realize she's been over a lot lately. The complex aroma of chili hits me when I open the front door. And could that be homemade bread?

"Hello, Kathleen," says Mom. She's at the counter, cutting a dark loaf of pumpernickel bread into thick slices.

"Hey, Kath," Nadia says. "How's it going?"

I'm tempted to say, "Well, Nadia, I'm a raving lunatic," but instead I say, "Fine."

Nadia pulls apart a head of lettuce and runs it under cold water. "I brought my famous chocolate cheesecake for dessert. And a bottle of wine."

"A bottle of wine?" My stomach feels like a meat grinder. "Uh, Nadia, would you help me get the good wineglasses?"

She follows me into the dining room, but I pull her into the living room instead. I want to be out of hearing distance of Mom.

"Nadia," I say, "that's a bad idea."

"Why? It's just wine."

"No, you don't get it. It starts with a glass of wine, and before you know it you're drinking coffee and brandy at seven-thirty in the morning."

"Kath, what are you talking about?"

"Mom. She'll start drinking. Big-time."

"What? She hardly ever drinks," Nadia says.

"She hasn't done it yet," I say, "but if you give her that wine it'll happen."

"How can you be so sure?" Nadia asks.

I clamp my teeth together to stop from answering. What can I tell her? I've seen it? She's already done it? Oh, yeah, and by the way, I'm insane. In fact, I barely know who I am today.

"Kath?" Nadia says quietly, "if you're worried, why not ask her?"

"I can't do that," I say. "She's my mother."

"All the more reason," says Nadia. "Honestly, I don't understand your family. You never talk about things. Even Nick didn't."

"What? You couldn't shut Nick up," I protest.

"Yeah," says Nadia. "He had a thousand funny stories. But did you guys ever talk about things that mattered?"

I open my mouth but nothing comes out. I try to think back to a serious conversation at the dinner table. I come up empty.

"Let's just ask her," Nadia says, heading for the kitchen. Before I can stop her, she says, "Mom?"

That irritates me all over again, her use of the word *Mom*.

Mom is pouring the chili into a big bowl. She finishes, then says, "Yes?"

"Kathleen has a problem with me bringing wine

for dinner," says Nadia. "She thinks you shouldn't have any."

"Oh, dear," Mom says. The color drains out of her face, leaving her unnaturally pale. She leans back against the kitchen counter. "I had a bit of a problem in college, you know, with drinking? I nearly flunked out of my junior year because of it. I got myself straightened out, though. That's why I rarely drink now."

"Oh, Mom," Nadia says, giving her a hug.

Mom's eyes get teary. "I've even thought, oh, in the last week, even thought of going out and buying a bottle. So far I haven't, but—"

"And you won't," says Nadia. "I'll put this back in the car."

"No, that's okay," Mom says. "We'll have it with dinner."

"But—" I say.

"Just one glass, Kathleen," Mom says. "In Nick's memory."

I'm so nervous at dinnertime that my throat closes up. I can't eat.

Mom pours wine all around, raises her glass, and says, "To Nick."

We are all misty eyed as we clink glasses, but at least no one starts crying. I don't think I could take that.

"Great chili," says Nadia.

"Is this homemade bread?" asks Dad.

That's about the end of the conversation, until Mom clears her throat and says, "I'm taking a bit of time off work."

"I'm sorry. What did you say?" I ask.

"I've been giving it some thought," she says. "I've asked the library for a leave of absence. There are more important things than working."

Dad looks as stunned as I feel. "What will you do with your time?" he finally asks.

"I'm not sure," Mom says.

Drink, I think frantically. Drink coffee and brandy for breakfast. Schlep around in your housecoat. Make dinner from a box. I push chili around on my plate and shred my bread into little pieces.

"I might do volunteer work," Mom says. "Maybe get caught up on all the things I've let go. And there's that novel I've always wanted to write." She sips her wine. "But first, spring cleaning, and maybe a new coat of paint all around."

"I'll come over first thing in the morning to help," Nadia says.

Sure, I think. Why not? You're over all the time as it is.

For the rest of dinner, Mom and Nadia make plans. Spring cleaning first, then paint the kitchen, then wallpaper the bathroom. I listen without much interest. Mostly I'm watching to see how much wine Mom drinks. To my relief she takes only a few sips. When Dad finishes his glass, she offers him the rest of hers.

I'm so relieved that I manage to choke down a tiny bite of Nadia's chocolate cheesecake. After, I offer to help with dishes, but Nadia says breezily, "Oh, that's okay. Mom and I will do them."

I wander into Nick's room, drawn there by my memories of him. It occurs to me that Nick was irreplaceable.

Me? Obviously, not so much.

Shards

Something wakes me up in the middle of the night. A noise maybe? I roll over and put my pillow over my head.

What? Wait. My pillow? What am I doing in my own bed? Wearing my pajamas? Oh, please, tell me this isn't happening. I had fallen asleep in Nick's bed, I was sure of it. I'd gone into Nick's room after dinner. I remember picking up the framed photo of him and Nadia taken last Christmas. I'd stifled the urge to smash it, and carefully replaced it on his dresser.

And then I'd picked it back up. I raised it up over my head, and threw it down. Hard.

It bounced on the soft carpet, mocking me.

So I carried the photo into the bathroom. It made a satisfying sound as it hit the tiled floor.

I'd gone back into Nick's room, careful not to step on the glass, touching the things he had loved: his pennants on the wall, his old teddy bear, his beer mug collection. I picked up my least favorite mug, the one that sported a humongous pair of breasts on the front. One of Nick's friends had given it to him on his twenty-first birthday. Nick called it "the mug with jugs."

Typical Nick humor, which, at the time, had annoyed me.

I remember putting the mug back, then going into his closet. I'd pulled a shirt off a hanger, thinking to sleep in it, but it smelled like fabric softener. Feeling like a pervert, I fished a T-shirt out of his dirty clothes hamper. It still smelled of Nick's deodorant. I'd put it on, thinking *how sick is this? Wearing my dead brother's dirty clothes?*

I'd thought about going back to my own room. That would be the sensible thing to do. It was certainly not sensible, or sane, to curl up on Nick's bed. Clutching his teddy bear, I eventually fell asleep.

And here I am, at two in the morning, in my own bed, in my own pajamas, awake and thirsty. I stagger toward the bathroom. At the last second, I remember the smashed photo and the broken glass. I turn on the light.

It's gone. No photo. No shards of glass. The floor tiles are perfectly clean.

My mouth goes even drier. There, lying on the counter, is a toothpaste tube.

Scrunched in the middle. Just like Nick always left it.

For one insane moment, I think, *he's back. Nick is back.*

Oh, man, I'm losing it. I put my hand on the connecting door that leads to Nick's room. I'm ready to throw it open, rush in, check the bed.

No. That's giving in to insanity. He's not there. He's gone. Dead, dead, more than dead.

I drink a glass of water and go back to bed. My *own* bed.

Multiple Copies

And wake up in Nick's. I'm wearing his T-shirt and hugging his teddy bear. I dash into the bathroom, see the glass on the tiled floor, and skid to a halt just in time.

On the counter, there's the toothpaste tube, just the way I like it, smooth and ready to squeeze from the bottom. Had it been a dream? Finding a scrunched toothpaste tube?

For a moment, I think I might be sick. It had seemed so *real*. But I bet the crazy guy in town thinks his invisible friend is real, too.

Enough. If I'm not crazy yet, I'm going to drive myself there.

Ha. Like I'd drive myself anywhere.

Feeble joke. Not funny. Stick to routine. What do sane people do when they wake up? Oh, yeah. Clean up the glass on the bathroom floor, have a shower, eat breakfast.

Then go crazy.

I'm climbing out of the shower when I hear voices in Nick's room. I get dressed, and open the door to find Nadia and Mom standing amidst a bunch of boxes.

"What are you doing?" I ask, although it is perfectly clear what they are doing.

"We have to move on," Mom says, folding a football jersey and placing it in a box.

Move on?

"No, not that one," I say, retrieving the jersey. I claim other things—Nick's University of Wisconsin–Eau Claire sweatshirt, the scarf I knitted for him last year, his mug with jugs, several pennants. I take these bits of Nick back to my room and sit on my bed, hugging them to me. I hear Mom and Nadia calmly discussing what to do with the rest and I can't stand it, I can't.

I grab my coat and escape.

I'm walking aimlessly, my only goal to put distance between me and the dismantling of Nick's life. Thick flakes of snow drift down from the sky, landing with a sigh on the evergreens and hedges. It must be snowing at the cemetery, too, covering the mound of Nick's grave with a thick cloak of forgetfulness. Can he hear the snow fall? Does he feel the cold?

We have to move on.

Is Mom that eager to get rid of Nick? That quick to erase his life? It's like stripping the beds when company leaves. Oh, look, Nick's gone. Let's strip his room. Let's make believe he was never here.

What does she need the room for, anyway? A guest bedroom? An office? Or maybe she'll rent it out to some college student, someone who looks a little like Nick. Dark hair and gray eyes and a ready laugh.

Or maybe she'll invite Nadia to move in. Why not? She's here half the time anyway. Wouldn't be much of a change.

I'm so lost in my thoughts that I don't hear the car that pulls up and paces me. No, not a car. A van, with lettering that says it belongs to Jay's Place.

It's Luke.

"Need a ride?" he asks.

I hesitate. The seconds drag. The snow falls, covering my hair, melting down my neck.

"It's okay, Kathleen," says Luke. "You've fought this battle with yourself before, remember?"

"That was Kate."

His eyes light up. "Kate? You call her Kate? And who is Kate, if not you?"

"You remember her?" I ask, excited. If he remembers Kate then she was real, not a figment of my psychotic mind.

"Short blue hair, funky clothes, rotten attitude? Who could forget her?" he says, smiling. "Listen, come for breakfast with me. I know this place where the chef does amazing things to an omelet."

"Why should I trust you?" I ask.

"Because Kate did."

I *must* be crazy, because I get into the van. It looks and smells new—no fast food wrappers or coffee cups or other debris.

Luke seems nervous. I'm not sure what gives me that impression. His hands maybe, gripping the wheel as if he expects it to take over. We drive through town, past the restaurants on Main Street, but we don't stop. By the time we reach the town limits, I'm thinking panic might be a good option. Was Jen right about him? *Where is he taking me?*

Then Luke turns into the parking lot of a restaurant. Jay's Place. The name on the van. I hop out, hoping the snow will cool my burning face.

"We'll need the key," Luke says, reaching past me to unlock the door.

"You work here?"

"In this reality, I do."

In this reality?

I'm wondering what he means by that, but I'm too apprehensive to ask. What if he's as crazy as I am? I'll lose the one bit of stability I have left in my life.

We walk past cozy booths and small tables decorated with hurricane lamps. Jay must be a nautical buff, judging from the ropes, lobster traps, and paintings of fishing boats. Luke leads me through a swinging door into the kitchen. Everything is stainless steel. Everything is spotless. He gestures to a small table in the corner of the kitchen. I sit down and take off my coat.

He washes his hands and gets to work, pulling several large oranges out of the industrial-sized fridge. A moment later, he produces fresh-squeezed orange juice. It tingles on my tongue, a wonderful blend of tart and sweet.

I watch him prepare the omelet, mesmerized by his hands. He breaks eggs one-handed, chops ham, onion, and cheese with a gigantic chef's knife, whips the eggs with a wire whisk. He moves with the ease of long practice, and delivers a perfect omelet, complete with a slice of orange on the side.

"Eat up before it gets cold," he says.

I take a bite. To my relief, I manage to swallow. No side order of guilt, here. I have another bite, and another. I even eat the orange slice.

"You were right," I say. "The chef here does amazing things with omelets."

Luke's face creases into a smile. He looks younger, certainly no older than twenty. He joins me, carrying his own omelet. "Yeah, one day I'll own this place, and open it up for breakfast."

I let him finish his omelet before I ask the question that's driving me nuts. "What did you mean by '*in this reality*'?"

He starts a pot of coffee before he answers.

"You wake up in the morning and everything's changed, am I right?" He sits down at the table. His hands are folded in front of him. Large hands. Competent hands. I want to trust him, I do.

"You seem to have two different memories of the past few days," he goes on. "You wonder if you're going crazy."

My heart speeds up. "How did you know?"

"It's the same thing I went through," he says. "There's a perfectly logical explanation."

"Which is?"

He gets up, pours coffee. I add cream to mine, and wait. He nibbles on a nail, stalling.

"Multiple universes," he finally says.

This is *not* what I expected. I react by laughing out loud.

"You're joking, right?" I ask.

"Nope," he says. "It can all be explained by quantum mechanics. Particles can exist in more than one place at one time. So can we. Multiple universes."

"How many?"

"An infinite number. Some nearly identical to this one, where we are having this same conversation word for word. Only, with slight differences. You might have a tomato slice, instead of an orange garnish."

I glance down at the orange rind on my plate.

"Or," Luke continues, "in another universe, you didn't get in my car. You're still trudging through the snow."

I close my eyes, trying to make sense of his words. Multiple universes? Does he really think I'm that gullible, that I'll believe him?

"Would you care for some pie?" Luke asks.

His abrupt transition catches me by surprise. "Pardon me?"

"Pie. Would you like some?"

"Isn't pie for breakfast kind of decadent?" I ask.

"You ate your eggs," he replies with a shrug. "Apple or cherry?"

"Apple."

He brings a pie out of the fridge and cuts two large slices. "Cheddar cheese on top?"

"On apple pie?"

"Don't knock it till you try it," he says, placing a slice of Cheddar on top of my pie.

To my surprise, it's good. The sharpness of the Cheddar complements the sweetness of the apples.

"So, where did all these multiple universes come from?" I ask, playing along. "Do they just pop into existence?"

"Pretty much." Luke grabs a pen and a paper napkin. "There are several theories, but this one is the easiest to explain. The splitting universe theory."

"Which is?"

"Imagine a tree, with branches that split, again and again." He draws a tree: central trunk, a split partway up, each branch dividing into smaller and smaller branches.

"And why," I ask, "does this tree split?"

"Ever hear of the double-slit experiment?" he asks. "You take a beam of light and aim it at a piece of paper with two narrow holes cut in it. Behind that, catching the light, is photographic paper. Guess what happens?"

"I know this one," I say, leaning forward. "We learned it in Physics. Light acts like a particle and a wave. You get an interference pattern, bars of light and dark, on the paper."

"Exactly!" says Luke, as happy as if he'd discovered this himself. "And when you send just a single photon at a time through, what happens?"

I shake my head. We didn't cover that in Physics. Either that, or I forgot.

"The same thing. Exactly the same pattern of interference."

"But how can a single photon create an interference pattern?" I ask. "It can't interfere with itself."

"Unless," says Luke, "unless that single photon goes through both slits in the paper. You see what that means? It exists in two places, simultaneously. It travels through *both* slits at exactly the same time."

He gets up, paces, grabs the coffeepot, sets it down on the table.

"So if that's what's happening on the quantum level, it has to be happening on our level. Multiple universes. Splitting and re-splitting, like the branches of a tree. Every decision you make creates a split in the universe." He taps a split in the tree. "Now you exist in two universes, each of which will continue to split every time you make a new choice. There are multiple copies of us right now, eating apple pie in one universe, cherry in another."

"Peach in another?" I'm beginning to half believe him. Or, at least suspend my disbelief.

"No, never peach," he says, sitting back down. "I hate peach pie."

"In this universe you do."

"Trust me," he says. "Some things are immutable."

"Trying to impress me?" I joke.

"Depends. Is it working?" He pulls his chair closer. Our knees touch. My heart stutters.

"Totally." I take another bite of pie, trying to hide my reaction.

"Oh, man," he says softly, "I was dreading this."

My heart goes from stutter to slam. Dreading this? Dreading what? My attraction to him? Am I that obvious? Did my face give me away?

But then he says, "I was so afraid you'd think I was a crackpot and would walk right out that door. I wanted to tell you earlier, but your friend . . . uh . . ."

"Jen," I supply. My heart's beating so hard I can hear it echo in my ears.

"Yes, Jen. She doesn't like me, does she?"

"She thinks you're stalking me," I admit.

"I'm sorry. I should have explained earlier, but I was afraid you wouldn't believe me. I knew, after your first shift, that you were like me. *A traveler between realities.*"

My mouth goes dry. I gulp my coffee. "How did you know?"

He answers with a question. "Have you ever noticed something peculiar about me? And no jokes, please, about my appearance. I know I'm not much to look at."

What, is he kidding? Fishing for compliments? Okay, so he's heavy, but he's solid, he's *there*. But how do I say that without being insulting? Like if someone said, oh yeah, your mismatched eyes make you pretty, would I believe them?

So, I stick to the facts. "I sometimes see a shimmer in the air around you. And a few times, I thought you looked phase-shifted, like an image seen through cheap glasses. It's like seeing double, but not quite."

"Exactly. We don't physically jump between universes. Just our awareness shifts, moving between copies of ourselves."

I think about that for a bit, wonder what all the other "me's" are doing right then. For all I know, one "me" might be helping Mom and Nadia clean out Nick's room. Another "me" might have forbidden them to touch Nick's things.

"Okay, let's say you're right," I say. "We're shifting between multiple copies of ourselves. Is that why I have two sets of memories? The memories I carry with me when I shift, and the memories of the body I've just shifted into?"

"Exactly," Luke says.

I shiver. "We're like ghosts, possessing our own bodies for a time and moving on."

Luke reaches over and gives my hand a reassuring squeeze.

I'm starting to believe him. Either he's making sense, or we're both insane. What's that called? Two people sharing the same psychosis? I can't remember.

But then I do remember something that makes me feel a little dizzy. The piece of paper with his phone number on it. I'd put it in my purse. That much I was sure of. But the next time I'd looked, it was gone.

I'd shifted to a timeline where he hadn't given me the note. I don't know whether to be relieved, since I'm not losing my mind, or to be terrified, because shifting is even weirder.

Maybe my emotions show on my face.

"Scared?" Luke asks.

"Yes."

"I was too," he says, "when it started happening to me."

I feel a rush of gratitude. He's looking out for me. Showing up in my reality, after I shift. And then it hits me. How is he doing it?

"How do you follow me?" I ask him.

"Huh?" he says, chewing on a nail.

"Well, you're *here*, now, but you were also *there* when I was Kate. How do you find me?"

He goes to work on a second nail. "I don't know," he answers. "It's like I get pulled along with you."

"Oh, wow. I'm sorry," I say.

"Nothing to be sorry for." He gives my hand another squeeze.

We stay like that for a minute, my hand in his. I'm entranced by him, by his voice, by the way he looks straight at me, not at the bridge of my nose or my brown eye or my green eye, but straight at me. His eyes remind me of the night sky, black-black but with a glimmer of starlight.

"More pie?" he asks, breaking the mood.

I surprise myself by saying yes. He slides another slice over to me and takes more for himself. I'm thinking about what he said, about shifting between multiple universes.

"Why us? Why do *we* shift?" I lift my head to look up at Luke.

"I think everyone shifts a little, only they have no awareness of shifting, no carryover of memories. They dismiss the small changes in their world, find logical explanations. Like when you *know* you left your car keys on the counter, but then find them in a drawer."

"Or, you're sure you returned a book to the library, but you find it under your bed?" I suggest.

"Exactly."

I've been eating my second slice of pie as we talked. I look down, surprised to see I've finished it.

"So why *us*?" I ask. "Why are *we* aware of the differences?"

He answers with a question. "When did it start?"

"My brother's death," I answer, tapping the picture of the tree. I'm pointing to the first branch, where the tree trunk split in two.

"And for me," he says, "it started with my parents' deaths."

"But why would . . . ?" My voice trails off as I stare at the branching tree. "We're trying to find them, aren't we? Find a universe where they're alive?"

"Unconsciously, yes. At least that's my theory," Luke says.

"That makes absolutely no sense," I argue. "Lots of people suffer traumas. Why don't they remember shifting? Why have I never heard of this happening to anyone?"

"Is it really the sort of thing you tell people?" he asks.

I think about my cousin, the one who ended up in the psychiatric hospital.

"Or," he goes on, "maybe we're special. I mean, people have differing abilities. One person has perfect pitch, another is tone-deaf. One person may see the world in hues that most of us can't even dream of, and another is color blind. Maybe we're able to carry our memories with us. Or maybe we're making bigger jumps than most people, creating bigger changes in our worlds. Maybe that forced us into awareness."

I'm thinking about that, and looking at the tree he's drawn. How many times have I shifted since the night of the party? How many universes have I passed through? How far have I jumped?

And *that's* when it hits me. "Luke, I can go back. To the night of the party."

"The party?" Luke frowns.

"Yes. That's how Nick died. I went to this party with Jen and she got drunk and I called Nick to pick us up. And another car smashed into him." Tears sting my eyes at the memory.

"It was an accident, Kathleen. No one's fault," Luke says gently.

"It was *my* fault. If I hadn't gone to the party, he'd still be alive."

"You can't go back. Time moves forward like a river. You can't swim against the current."

"Fine, so I'll go sideways. To here," I say, touching a branch on the other side of the tree.

"It's not under your control, Kathleen. It's random."

"I don't believe you. You're making this up." I'm suddenly furious with him and his know-everything attitude.

"If I were making this up, wouldn't I come up with a better story than this?" He draws back his hands, tucks them under his arms. His breathing is fast but his face is devoid of emotion. I've offended him. Again.

He glances at his watch. "It's late. I'll drive you home."

"It's not even noon," I protest.

"We open for dinner in five hours," Luke explains. "I need to start cooking."

He hands me my coat and pushes through the swinging door into the restaurant, holding it open for me.

I'm about to say "Don't bother," but that's something Kate would say. I'd like to think I'm a little more mature than she is.

The only sound on the way home is the windshield wipers, brushing away the thickly falling snow.

KAY

Shifted

I am awake. I lie in bed and wonder if I've shifted. I've developed a game. I count two points if I know where I am without opening my eyes. Five points if I can do it with only one sense, like smell or sound. I can't hear the shower running and I don't smell coffee. I'm not sure where or who I am, but I give myself one point for effort.

I'm hungry. I have the oddest craving for tabbouleh. Aha! I'm Kate. I reach up to touch my hair. Oh, yeah. I'm a genius. Since hunger isn't technically one of the five senses, I award myself six points just to be generous.

Whoa, and I'm sleeping naked. That's a new one. I get up and find another surprise. A belly ring! Whoohoo, Kate, way to go. I didn't feel a thing, ha ha.

This is awesome. I'm not sure what state my

parents will be in, but I don't really care. So what if Mom is drinking? I'll go to Sunny's. Escape. I'm good at that.

I shower and towel-dry my hair. Sure beats blow-drying it each day. I peer critically at the color. Might be time for a touchup. The rich blueness is fading.

I'm wondering what to pierce next, maybe my eyebrow, when it hits me. I'm doing the double memory thing again. I clearly remember being Kathleen on Saturday, watching Luke cook an omelet, talking about multiple universes and shifting between them. On Sunday, I stayed home and caught up on schoolwork.

But I can tap into my new body's memories, Kate's memories. On Sunday, Kate had gone with Sunny to a tattoo/piercing parlor. She'd given a guy named Max a forged note from Mom, saying she had permission.

After that, Sunny and I had gone shopping. I look in my closet and there are the clothes: pre-torn jeans, a long-sleeved black T-shirt to wear under a white sweater that is mostly air.

I get dressed, pleased that the T-shirt comes down far enough to hide my piercing from my mother's eyes. But I shouldn't have worried. Her bedroom door is closed. I figure she's asleep. Very asleep, to judge from the amount of vodka that is gone from the bottle she bought yesterday. How can a person drink most of a bottle in one day? I remember Dad ordering in Chinese food last night, then retreating to the den.

But wait. Am I really on Kate's timeline? Or had the timeline split again, just after I dyed my hair? I have conflicting memories.

"Don't you think this is a little irresponsible?" Dad had asked. "Your mother doesn't need this right now."

Kate was about to say something like, "I don't need this shit either," but she knew her father would go ballistic if she spoke like that to him.

"I'm sorry," Kate said. "I didn't do it to upset her."

And Kate had given in, had asked her mother if she needed help with dinner.

But this body, this *new* one I've shifted into, remembers it differently.

"Don't you think this is a little irresponsible," Dad had asked. "Your mother doesn't need this right now."

That pissed me off. Has she paid any attention to my feelings since Nick died? No. Not even once.

So I said, "I don't need this shit either. Can't you see what's happening? She's turned into a total drunk, and you're too chicken to confront her."

Dad's eyes went a metallic gray. "Since when is it your job to criticize your mother? Or me, for that matter?"

"Get out of my room!" I yelled.

He glared at me, jaw muscles twitching. Then he turned and walked out, quietly shutting the door. It was as loud as a slam.

Since then, Dad hasn't spoken to me, except to ask, "Pork-fried rice or the house special?" So I'm not Kate. I'm someone else. Call me Kay.

I pour cereal into a bowl and add milk, but the milk comes out in glops. I pour it down the sink, recoiling at the smell. A quick hunt in the fridge reveals moldy Cheddar cheese, greenish sliced ham, and a few shriveled apples. I eat cold fried rice, house special, and run to catch the school bus.

Welcome to Kay's world.

The Open Road

I'm at lunch, staring at the tree Luke drew, when Sunny and Weed join me.

"Art class?" Sunny asks, looking at the drawing.

"Multiple universes," I explain.

"Coolness," says Weed. He puts his head down on the table and appears to fall fast asleep. I look at Sunny.

"He's wasted," she says. "So what's this about multiple universes?"

"What if," I say, "you were shifting between

alternate universes? Like in one, you have cereal for breakfast. Only, in a different universe, you have eggs. And in another universe, you eat cold fried rice?"

Sunny laughs. "You been smoking the good stuff?"

"Yeah. Got tired of the stuff Weed sells us." I paste a weak smile on my face. I'd half hoped she'd believe me. Or at least show some interest in the idea.

"So, speaking of which, want to come over tonight?" Sunny asks.

"Sure." Why not? There's nothing for me at home.

Dad orders pizza for dinner. We "dine" in front of the TV. Dad has three slices. I barely choke down two bites. Mom picks at hers, selecting a slice of mushroom and washing it down with a generous amount of vodka. She puts an olive in the glass and calls it a martini. Nobody laughs.

I'm furious with my father. Why doesn't he confront her? Why does he pretend that everything is normal? It's obvious that he's upset, since he barely speaks to Mom. So why is he such a wimp? Pretending a problem doesn't exist doesn't make it go away. He's the adult here. Why isn't he acting like one?

I refrigerate the leftover pizza, throw out our paper plates, and then take off for Sunny's. Snow falls in fat, wet flakes. Sunny's mom greets me at the door. She's dressed casually, in jeans and a sweater. She looks normal. Somehow, I'd expected her to be unusual, like Sunny.

We go up to Sunny's room. It's retro, with black lights and glowing posters, lava lamps and globe lamps with static electricity arcing across them. She lights some incense, then offers me a pipe full of weed. We sit together on her window seat, windows cranked open, and wave the smoke outside. I inhale deeply, the way she taught me, hold the smoke in my lungs, then exhale. Pretty soon, we're trashed.

"I should learn to drive," I announce. "I should."

"Okay," Sunny agrees. "Let's go."

"What? Now? Like this?"

"Sure," she says. "I'll take you over to the school. You can practice in the parking lot."

I figure that's safe enough. The school is only a few miles away. Sunny looks fine to drive. And I'm feeling mellow. Maybe that's best. Learn to drive when you are nice and relaxed. Play it safe. Stay in the parking lot. Yeah. I can handle that.

"We're going out for ice cream," Sunny calls down the hall to her mom.

"Be careful," says her mom from the studio. "It's snowing."

A good two inches of fresh, wet snow decorates Sunny's car. Laughing, we slide down the sloped driveway, using our shoes like skis. I slip and fall in slow motion. I brace myself for a jarring impact, but when I hit the pavement I feel nothing much at all. The wet snow soaks my jeans, but I can't feel that either. I'm wrapped in a layer of insulation as we drive to the school.

I have a small moment of panic as Sunny slides out at the first intersection. I look around, anticipating a car coming from the other direction. But we're alone on the road. Sunny spins the tires as we start again. The back of the car slides a little and then grips.

"Okay," she says, once we arrive at the school parking lot. "Switch."

As I get into the driver's seat I feel none of my usual anxiety. It's like I've stepped outside myself and am observing from a distance.

"Okay, this is an automatic, so it should be easy. The right pedal is the gas and the left pedal is the brake," Sunny says.

I'm thinking, I know all that. I took Driver's Ed at school. I start to tell her that, but what slips out of my mouth is, "Gas, go. Brake, stop."

She giggles, so I make it into a song. I step on the gas, singing, "Gas, go," then stomp on the brake, singing, "Brake, stop." I spin the wheels on "go" and slide a dozen or so feet on "stop."

We lurch around the parking lot for a bit, then Sunny says, "Okay, you're ready for the open road."

"Roger that, Roger," I say.

"Ten four, good buddy," she says.

I'm pulling out of the school parking lot when it occurs to me that I'm not exactly acting responsibly. I should stop the car and let Sunny drive us home, I should. I'm about to stop the car when I think of something else. Sunny's been smoking too. She's as stoned as I am. In fact, I'm probably the better driver right now, since I'm newer at it. New drivers are extra cautious.

I turn right, heading for Sunny's house. The road is wet, but not slippery. I drive a good five miles under the limit. A car comes toward me and I feel my heart speed up, but I keep to my own lane and the other car safely passes by.

"Slow down for the turn," Sunny cautions.

"Got it," I assure her. I slow down before making a right into her subdivision. The road is snow-covered here, due to less traffic, so I take my time and crawl along. And then it happens. A dark shape darts out of a driveway.

"D-dog!" shouts Sunny.

I tromp down with my right foot. But I hit the gas. The car leaps forward. Sunny yells. I hit the brake. Hard. The rear of the car slides sideways. I'm heading for the ditch, frantically trying to remember how to steer out of a skid. I pump the brakes, but we keep sliding. I turn the steering wheel. We change direction, now heading for a mailbox on the far side of the road.

Crunch! It's an awful sound, the rear side of the car knocking down the mailbox. We keep sliding, right into the ditch, and come to rest at an angle. I'm shaking so hard I can hardly breathe. I'm staring straight ahead, terrified of how Sunny might react.

The silence is very loud.

"Well, at least you didn't hit the dog," Sunny finally says.

Then she giggles. I start to laugh, and then I snort, sending Sunny into shrieks of laughter. She's holding her sides, tears rolling down her cheeks, shaking. As soon as one of us gets it under control, the other starts up again.

It's quite a while before we wind down.

Rescue

We finally get out and inspect the damage. We've snapped off the mailbox post about two feet off the ground. The mailbox lies crumpled in the ditch. A huge dent mars the back of Sunny's car.

"Do you think you can get it out of the ditch?" I ask.

Sunny shrugs. We get back in and she gives it a try, but only manages to dig us in deeper.

"We'll have to get pulled out," she says. "I don't want to call my mom. If she thinks I'm high, I'll be in major trouble."

"I have an idea." I'm remembering how Luke gave me his cell number. Do I have the scrap of paper in this reality? I check my purse. *Yes!* I pull out my phone and punch in the numbers.

"Hello," he says.

"Luke. It's me. Kay. I'm in trouble."

"Where are you?"

He arrives in less than ten minutes, driving the Jay's Place van. He looks bulky in his winter jacket, solid and real. I introduce him to Sunny. He nods hello, then turns to get towing ropes from his van. It takes only a moment to pull Sunny's car back onto the road.

"Can you make it home?" he asks her.

"No problem. I live half a block that way." She points to the street that I had been about to turn onto.

"I'll follow you," he says.

"That's okay," she says. "I'll drive Kay home first."

"No," says Luke. "I'll take Kay. You go straight home. I'll follow you."

Meekly, Sunny agrees. There's something in Luke's voice that doesn't leave room for argument.

"Thanks, Sunny," I say as I give her a hug. She hugs back, whispers in my ear, "He's hot!"

We follow Sunny home and see her safely inside. Our tires swoosh through the wet snow as Luke drives the short distance to my house.

"Here you go," he says in a curt voice.

"You're pissed at me," I say.

"No, I'm not."

"Don't patronize me."

He sighs. "Fine. You want me to say it? You're stoned. What did you think you were doing? Do you have any idea what might have happened?"

Now *that's* the wrong thing to say. Who does he think he is? My big brother? My Dad?

"Since when do you have the right to run my life?" I argue.

"Since you called me for help."

"Well, next time I won't."

"Fine," he says.

"Fine," I say.

I slam the door as I get out. I think I hear a faint "You're welcome," but I ignore it. My last thought, before I go to sleep is: it doesn't matter. With any luck, I'll shift during the night. Let Kay clean up the mess I'll leave behind.

KATHLEEN

Falling

I'm not even out of bed before I call him.

"Hello," he says in a sleepy voice.

"Did I wake you up?"

"Yes." I hear him yawn.

"I'm sorry. I couldn't wait to talk to you. I'm so sorry for last night. Kay can be pretty stupid at times."

There's a long silence, then, "You *are* Kay, remember?"

I greet that with a long silence of my own.

"Now you're the one who's angry with me," Luke says. "Look, why don't I drive you to school?"

I'm thinking, sure, like I want a lecture about responsibility. But what I say is, "No, go back to sleep. I think Jen might be picking me up."

"I'll pick you up after school, then. We can go skating at Pine Ridge Park. There's an outdoor rink."

"I don't know how to skate."

"I'll teach you."

"Don't you have to work?"

"I have the day off."

"Won't we get kinda cold?"

"Look, if you don't want to go, just say so," Luke says with a hint of irritation.

I don't want to go. I'm not a fan of winter sports. But I do have skates. Dad bought them for me, two Christmases ago. Dad often bought me things I didn't need or want: skates, cross-country skis, a snowboard. I'd rather get a root canal than go skating but I say, "Sure. Pick me up at three thirty. I've got skates."

"It's a date, then," he says. "I mean, not a *date* date. I mean . . ."

I'm grinning.

"Uh, three thirty," he says, and hangs up.

"I'm going skating after school with some friends," I tell Mom. She's at the table drinking coffee and reading the paper. I check my body's memory to find I'm in the timeline where Mom has quit work but isn't drinking.

"Will you be home by five?" she asks.

"Probably."

"Could you do me a favor then? I'll make a meat-loaf and leave it in the fridge. Would you throw it in the oven and bake a few potatoes to go along?"

"Sure. Where will you be?"

"At a mad meeting," she says. At least that's what I *think* I hear her say.

"Mad?"

"Mothers Against Drunk Driving. I'm going to a meeting in Eau Claire. I'm thinking of starting a MADD chapter here in Pine Ridge."

"But the guy who hit Nick wasn't drunk."

Mom wraps her hands around her coffee mug. "I know, Kathleen. But many, many other parents have lost family members to drunk drivers. I'd like to—oh, I don't know—maybe just get involved somehow. I'd like to think Nick's death counted for something."

I'm thinking, his *life* counted for something. But I don't say that. Instead I give Mom a hug. When I pull away, there are tears in her eyes.

The day goes by at a snail's pace. My thoughts keep drifting to Luke, to his dark eyes and kissable lips. Finally, three-thirty comes. He pulls up in his own car, the black Mini.

Maya, Steph, and Jen are there, watching. "Wow," says Jen. "He's adorable."

I elbow her gently and say, "Go find your own hunk. This one's mine."

He leans over to open the door. I climb in. It's warm, with the heater going full blast. I feel awkward, remembering my behavior of last night. I half expect him to lecture me, but all he says is, "How was your day?"

"Fine," I answer. "How was yours?"

"Fine," he says. "I've been looking forward to seeing you."

Oh, yeah.

We have the ice rink to ourselves. The sun, low in the sky, sends tree shadows across the surface of the ice. It looks like something out of a movie. Too pretty to skate on. But Luke already has his skates on and laced. He looks down at my pathetic efforts. My laces are uneven, like I've done them with my eyes closed.

"There's a technique," Luke says, "which you obviously don't have."

I'm about to get defensive, I mean, when have I had the chance to practice? But then I see he's grinning. And me, I'm content to be taken care of. I'm sitting on a wooden bench at the side of the rink. He's crouched down, patiently tugging at my laces. I see the top of his head. My fingers itch to run through his hair, dark and wavy. Is it as soft as it looks?

"How does it feel?" he asks.

What? Did he just read my mind? Then I realize he means the skates.

"Snug," I reply.

"Too snug?"

"I'm not sure. I don't know how they are supposed to feel."

"Try them out." He takes my gloved hands in his own and pulls me to my feet. My skates slither out from under me, and I fall into him.

It's a sweet moment, his arms around me, my body pressed against his. I imagine I can feel his warmth through our winter coats. We stay there for a second or two, then he helps me get my balance. He skates backward, holding my hands, while I totter unsteadily along.

"Having fun?" he asks.

"Tons." I'm not having fun with the skating part, but being with him makes up for that.

After a little, he lets go of me. I attempt to glide gracefully, but my skates have a mind of their own.

"My ankles hurt," I tell him.

"Let's take a break, then." We sit down on the bench, and he opens the knapsack he's brought along. Inside is a thermos of hot chocolate. He pours the steaming liquid into two cups and hands me one. Then he produces homemade cookies, fragrant with cinnamon and studded with raisins and nuts.

I bite into one. "Hmmm . . . I think I'm in love."

He gives me a startled look, then glances at the cookies. His face relaxes. "Yeah," he says. "Men make the best chefs."

We argue over that for a moment. It's nice,

arguing. Like old friends. Only it occurs to me that all I know is his first name.

"What's your last name?" I ask.

"Basso," he says. "It's Maltese for 'short.' Kind of ironic, isn't it?"

"Maltese?" I ask, smiling. He *is* short, not much taller than I am.

"From Malta. A set of islands in the Mediterranean. My parents were born there. Moved here before I was born."

"Oh," I say. "That explains your permanent tan."

"You should see me in the summer," he says, grinning. He touches my hair. "I like your hair better like this. I mean, I like it blue and spiky too, but it makes you look about twelve years old."

Mental note. Tell Kate to grow her hair back in. Kay, too. I move a little closer to him, so that our legs touch.

"Cold?" he asks.

I'm not, but I say, "Yes," hoping he'll put his arm around me. And he does. I lean back against him, my head nestled into his shoulder. When he speaks, I hear the rumble of his voice through his chest.

"You feel like talking about last night?" he asks.

I don't. Not really. Although I woke up this morning consumed with guilt, I've now been Kathleen for eight hours. Kay and her problems seem a universe apart from me. Which, in a way, they are. But I'm sure Luke will correct me if I say that. *You are Kay, remember?*

I'm not sure how Luke interprets my silence. Then he says, "I'm sorry I yelled at you last night. I've no right to judge you."

"You sounded like my brother, Nick," I admit. "Like the time he caught me playing with matches down in the basement. I was trying to make a fire for Barbie. She was camping with Ken." Luke chuckles, so I go on. "Nick went ballistic. Dragged me upstairs to see Mom, showed her the evidence. Mom cut me off TV for a week and banished me to my room. I told Nick I hated him."

"Did you? Hate him?"

"Nah. He smuggled a whole bag of chips to me later that evening."

Luke takes a long breath, lets it out slowly. "He sounds like a good brother."

"The best." My voice comes out in a whisper. "It's my fault, you know."

"We've been over this already," Luke says. "It was an accident, Kathleen."

"If I knew how to drive, I could have driven Jen and me back from that party," I tell him. "I should learn to drive, I should."

"So, you decided to start last night?"

"It seemed like a good idea at the time."

"Always does when you're high."

"Is that the voice of experience?" I ask.

"Yes."

"Want to tell me about it?"

"No."

"Why not?"

"I had some tough times after my parents died. Let's just leave it at that."

I feel let down. He doesn't trust me. Maybe he sees I'm upset, because a second later he says, "Why don't I teach you to drive?"

"My father tried. It was a total disaster."

"I'm not your father." Something in his voice makes me look up. My face is a short distance from his. I look from his eyes to his lips and back again. His head tilts down, a fraction closer. I hold my breath. A ridiculous thought springs to mind. Is my breath fresh?

The moment stretches out. He's going to kiss me. I know he is. Then his expression changes.

"You're so damn young." His arm lifts away from my shoulder. He's suddenly gone, a figure on the ice, a spring coiled tight and needing to unwind. I watch him speed skate around the rink, then reverse and skate backward, fluid despite his bulk. His shadow dances beside him, blue-black in the fading light of a January afternoon. He slides to a stop, sending slivers of ice into the still air.

"I'm not that young," I call out to him. "I'm almost eighteen."

In a few economical pushes of his skates he reaches me. "I'm twenty-three."

We don't talk much as Luke drives me home. It's only later that I realize I don't know anything about him.

Except that I'm falling in love with him.

KATE

Decision

I am awake. Someone snores softly beside me. I reach out my hand and touch Trojan's soft fur. He stirs and stretches, pushing his feet into the small of my back.

I check out my hair. It's spiky. I'm either Kate or Kay or some variation. Eyes closed, I search my body's memory. The Kate/Kay split had occurred when my father confronted me about my blue hair. I remember telling my father I hadn't meant to hurt Mom's feelings. I'd helped her make dinner. Okay, so I'm Kate.

Kay had been so angry. Correction, Kate had been angry. Kay had been pissed. Her dad didn't give a rat's ass about her. Hardly knew she existed. He'd lived for Nick, for his son, his wonderful football-playing son.

But today I am Kate. It won't be so bad. Mom will drown her sorrows in vodka, but Dad has come out of the den and is acting normal again. He occasionally picks up groceries after work, sometimes cooks dinner, even does dishes. And, unlike Kay's father, he's still talking to me.

I'm thinking of Luke as I go into the bathroom. I check out my hair, midnight brown and three inches high. Luke was right. I look twelve years old. I'll grow it out, I will.

So young, Luke said. He must see me as a child. Someone to protect, like a stray cat or an abused puppy.

And what is he to me? A big brother substitute? Someone to call when I screw up?

Yes. Those things. But more. So much more.

I shower and spike my hair. It's funny, since my brother has been gone a while, but I still lock the door that leads to his bedroom so he can't walk in on me. Old habits die hard.

Dad has left for work. Mom is still asleep. I rummage for food in the kitchen, but Dad forgot to get milk, so cereal is not an option. I check the freezer, but we are out of bagels too. I settle for a handful of peanuts. They're stale. Great. I hope Dad thinks to pick up a few things on his way home.

So damn young.

But young doesn't mean irresponsible. Doesn't

mean incapable. Doesn't mean you can't go buy your own milk. Pick up your own bagels. Maybe get your mother out of the house. Give her a reason not to drink for a few hours.

I write a note for Mom and leave it on the coffee-maker. It says, "Let's get groceries together after school."

I have to run to make the bus.

Her Turn Now

"Hi, honey," Mom says when I walk in the door after school. "Ready to go shopping?"

She's dressed in jeans and a sweater. She looks a little rough around the eyes, kind of puffy and gray, but she seems sober. I give her a hug. There's no hint of alcohol.

"Why don't I drive?" I ask.

"Oh, no, dear. I can drive," she says.

Okay, great, I've just screwed up. She thinks that I think that she's been drinking. Why else would I offer to drive? I've avoided every opportunity to drive for the last year, even with Dad hounding me to get my permanent license.

"Mom, I'd like to try. I need to learn *sometime*," I say. "I can go the back way, through the subdivisions."

"Oh," she says, brightening. "Oh! Of course."

The roads have been salted and are fine except for a thin rim of ice near the edge. I drive five below the speed limit and slow down way before each stop sign. When I get to the grocery store, I pull into a spot miles away from any other cars.

"Wow, we made it," I say as I turn off the ignition.

"You did great," Mom says.

"Yeah," I say. "But we'll never get the nail marks out of the armrests."

She glances down at the armrests, then laughs. I haven't heard her laugh since Nick died.

I've brought a shopping list, but we mostly go up and down the aisles, taking our time. We buy green beans and lettuce and onions and potatoes and squash. We choose cherries that come from Chile, and oranges the size of small grapefruits. Dad hasn't been great about buying fresh fruit or vegetables, so we add snap peas and asparagus. Mom grabs a cantaloupe and throws it into the cart.

I remember milk and cereal and bagels and cream cheese. Mom adds yogurt and eggs. We stock up on meat and fish, and we are done.

When we get home, I fill two glasses with iced tea and offer one to Mom. She licks her lips and I know she's thinking of having a drink. But she takes the iced tea.

"Thanks," she says.

We tackle the job of putting away the groceries.

Mom chugs her iced tea in record time, so I refill her glass before she can reach for something stronger. She gives me a look that says, *I know what you are doing*, but she drinks the tea just the same.

"Great dinner, girls," Dad says when we sit down to eat. We have boneless pork chops with sautéed mushrooms, green beans, and salad. For dessert, I bring out the cherries and coffee. Dad offers to clear and do dishes, which works for me.

And for some strange reason, which I don't quite understand, I eat everything on my plate. It's the first time I've really *eaten* at our dinner table since Nick died. It feels good, filling me in more ways than one.

I excuse myself to do homework. I have one nagging fear, that Mom will start pouring martinis after dinner.

But then I think, *I tried my best*. It's her turn now.

KAY

Ask Me if I Care

I'm so *pissed*. All that time spent shopping and there's not a friggin' thing in the house to eat.

I've shifted. This raises the definition of "sucks" to a new high. Dad's at work, Mom is asleep on the couch with an empty vodka bottle on the coffee table. I catch the bus to school, and I am not in my happy place.

It gets worse. In first hour, Math, I've forgotten to do my problem set. That's another big, fat zero for Kay. In Bio, we have a test. Kay didn't study. History is surprise quiz. I'm very surprised, which is not a good thing.

Lunchtime is a real pain in the ass. I can tell something's wrong with Sunny right away. She doesn't offer me her lunch.

"What's wrong?" I ask, alarmed. The last time I

was with Sunny she was laughing. That was the night of the accident. I'd swerved to avoid hitting a dog and hit a neighbor's mailbox instead. At the time, it had struck us both as hilarious. "At least you didn't hit the dog," Sunny had said. But right now, she doesn't look at all amused.

"Last night," she says, "the police paid a little *social* call. Seems that a neighbor called them with my license plate number. I'm now charged with destruction of property and failing to stay at the scene of an accident."

"Oh."

"At least they offered me Teen Court."

"What's Teen Court?"

"A court of your peers," Sunny says, making "*peers*" sound like a bad word. "The prosecuting attorney, defending attorney, and jury are all high school students."

"That's good, right? It's not even real court," I say.

"Look, maybe the attorneys and the jury are students, but the judge is real. I can still be convicted, and sentenced."

I'm thinking, *so, that's your problem, not mine.*

And then I think, *what am I turning into?*

"Look, I can pay for the mailbox," I offer.

"Great. Maybe you'd like to come to my house and deal with my mom."

"It was an accident, Sunny."

"Yeah. *Your* accident, remember?"

"You talked me into driving! You were the one who was all, let's go driving and it'll be fun, and oh, you're ready to tackle the real road now." That's Kay speaking. I try to stop her, but the words fly out of my mouth.

"I was high," Sunny says in a hissy voice.

"Great excuse, Sunny."

Sunny slams her fist down on the table. "You're impossible! I'm taking the rap for you. You could at least show some gratitude."

"Why don't you tell her the truth then? That I was driving?" That's Kathleen talking. Good old responsible Kathleen.

"My mom would kill me. It's the first rule. Don't let anyone else drive the car."

The whole thing pisses me off. It was her idea to get baked, her idea to let me drive. Why is she blaming this on me?

"I already offered to pay for the mailbox," I say again.

"Wow. How immensely generous." She stomps off, throws her lunch bag into a trash can. I watch her buy a burger, but instead of coming back, she sits a few tables away.

Fine. Let her be that way. Ask me if I care.

Escape

Over a week goes by. I'm still Kay. My life sucks to the nth degree. I've lost my only friend, Sunny, and now eat lunch alone. Just three tables away I see Jen, Maya, and Steph. Even Maya has stopped sending me sympathetic looks. Jen acts like I've never existed. I've been erased. Like Nick.

My home life is just as bad. When I get home from school, Mom is sitting on the couch, a drink at her side. She's in shapeless track pants and a sweat top. I don't think she's wearing a bra. Last night's dirty dishes are still stacked in the sink. Couldn't she have loaded the dishwasher? At the very least? I head into the kitchen for a soda. It smells like fish. I soon discover why—the remains of a tuna casserole, no doubt crawling with salmonella, sits on the stove.

"I'm going to Sunny's, okay?" I ask. "She invited me to sleep over."

"What about dinner?" Mom asks. She's talking in that overly careful voice again.

"We'll order in." I throw some clothes and toiletries into a bag. I grab the gym socks Weed gave me. Inside I find two joints. Good man, that Weed. I'll have to buy my own stuff from him now that Sunny is out of the picture. I put on my coat and go into the kitchen.

"I'm taking a few sodas," I call out.

"That's fine," says Mom.

I reach into the fridge, but don't grab the sodas. I grab a bottle of white wine, a one-and-a-half-liter jug. Mom will assume she drank it herself. At least there's some benefit to her blackouts.

The pack is heavy, but my spirits are light as I leave the house.

Three hours later, I spot the flaw in my plan. Luke doesn't answer his phone. I'm at the library, killing time, leaving one message after another. Just as I'm about to admit defeat and trudge back home, my cell phone vibrates. I head to the lobby to answer. Luke's voice is . . . well, it's like you're lost in the forest and you reach a road. You know if you follow it, it will lead you home.

"What's wrong?" Luke asks.

"Nothing," I say.

"And the truth would be?"

"Everything."

"Where are you?"

"The library."

"And then you will be going where?"

"Not home. Anywhere but home. Could I come to your place?"

Long pause. I count five seconds. "Look, Kay, it's Friday. Our busiest night. I can't leave."

"Yeah. No problem. I understand. It's okay." But my voice breaks up.

Short pause. "No. It's not okay. When does the library close?"

"Eleven."

"I'll be there."

Bad Influence

I'm waiting for eleven o'clock. I'm starving. I've drunk gallons of water from the fountain and have read every teen magazine that I can find.

What am I doing? I don't have a clue. I've got wine and weed in my knapsack. I also have my Tigger pajamas and my Scooby-Doo toothbrush. What this means in the great scheme of things, I have no clue.

The lights flash in the library. A voice comes over the speakers, giving the fifteen-minute warning. I leave at five to eleven.

He's waiting for me in the Jay's Place van. He reaches across the front seat and pops open the door. I slide in and put my knapsack at my feet. I smell something wonderful, and my mouth waters.

"Ribs?" I ask.

"Uh-huh," he says in a smug-chef voice. "Ribs, Caesar salad, turtle cheesecake."

"I've died and gone to heaven," I declare. "Are you okay about leaving work?"

He gives me a quick look, then pulls out onto the road. "I'm covered. It's fine."

Something in his voice tells me it's not fine. I've just screwed up. I've acted like a kid, calling for help.

"Luke, why don't you just take me home?"

"It's *fine*. I've got it covered."

His apartment is tiny. Galley kitchen, not big enough for two people to work in without stepping on each other. L-shaped living/dining room. There's a narrow hallway that I expect leads to a single bedroom and a bath.

"Excuse the mess," Luke says as we enter.

Mess? Oh, there it is. A laundry basket on the couch, loaded with precisely folded clothes.

"Pigsty," I say. "You need a cleaning lady."

He flashes me a broad smile.

I throw my coat onto the couch. He picks it up and hangs it in the hall closet. I look down to see my shoes making a puddle on the parquet floor. I kick them off, set them on the mat beside the door. I grab a paper towel from the kitchen, wipe up the melted snow, and hunt for the garbage pail.

"Under the sink." He turns on the oven, puts the foil-wrapped ribs in to heat. He opens the fridge and sets the salad and cheesecake inside. In the few seconds he has the fridge open I notice two things: it is very clean and very nearly empty.

He catches my eye. "I'm not home much."

"Am I that transparent?" I ask.

"Yes." He smiles. "Would you like a drink? Soda? Juice?"

"Oh!" I suddenly remember. I fish the wine out of my knapsack and hold it up for him to see. "I brought this."

Time stops. I can't read his face. I'm holding my breath.

"I don't drink, Kay," he says. "And you are way too young to start."

Well, that settles it. I'm not that young. Almost eighteen. Old enough to decide for myself.

"Do you have a corkscrew?" I ask.

"No." He says it in a flat voice.

I count to ten, then realize the wine comes with a screw top. I open it, look through his cupboards. There are no wineglasses, so I grab two tumblers. I half fill them, and hand him one.

"No."

"Why not?"

"It's complicated."

"So? Explain. I have time."

"So damn young," he says.

But he lifts his glass in a salute and takes a sip.

"It's like this," he says, about an hour later.

We've eaten the ribs and salad. We've had coffee and cheesecake. He does everything with flair.

Parsley on the ribs, lemon wedges on the side of the Caesar salad, mint leaves on top of the cheesecake.

"I'm afraid of losing control," he says.

"Like my mother," I say. "Coffee and brandy for breakfast. Vodka with an olive for dinner."

"No. Not like that. I mean when I get drunk there's no telling what universe I'll shift into."

He leads the way into the living room. We sit on opposite sides of the couch and drink our wine. I'm on my second glass and feeling light-headed. He's on his first glass, but it's down to dribbles. I pour more. He tries to put his hand over the glass, but I'm quicker.

"It's like the old cliché," he says. "You know, going to bed drunk and waking up the next morning not knowing where you are. But in my case, it's happened. I end up who knows where. I worry that one day, if I'm not careful, I'll shift so far away that I'll never find my way back to where I want to be."

"And where would that be?" I hold my breath and wait for him to answer.

"Here," he says.

I don't know what to say. His eyes, calm and steady, are fixed on mine. I don't know how to feel. I don't know how I want this night to end. I'm not even sure who I am anymore. The moment goes on too long; gets too intense.

He looks away first, chewing his lower lip.

I change the subject, hoping to alleviate the awkwardness of the moment.

"Do you ever wonder what happens when your awareness shifts out of a body?" I ask. "What's left? A zombie?"

He laughs. "Well, then, there'd be a lot of zombies floating around in the universe. Universes, that is." He sips his wine. "No, I think when our awareness shifts out, the person that's left behind simply goes on, living their own life."

"Does it retain our memories of shifting?"

"I doubt you remember what happened when the other person was in control. The mind protects itself. Otherwise, we'd go crazy."

"Or maybe, like my cousin, the mind didn't do such a great job of protecting itself," I say.

"Cousin?"

"He ended up in a psychiatric hospital. Multiple personalities. I thought, at first, I was following in his footsteps."

"I'm sorry," Luke says, taking another taste of his wine. His glass is half-empty. I move over to sit next to him and refill it.

"Hey, you're going to get me drunk," he warns.

"Not on two glasses of wine," I say. "Even I'm not drunk on two glasses."

"And here I was worried about corrupting a minor. Look who's corrupting whom." He smiles, but it's a sad smile. "I didn't mean for this to happen. To get involved with you."

"Nick would appreciate it," I say. "You looking out for me."

"I guess." He drinks his wine and sighs. "Man, I miss smoking when I drink."

I jump up. I fish in my knapsack and triumphantly pull out the two joints that Weed supplied. I set one down on the coffee table and find the matches I've brought.

"I didn't mean that kind of smoking," Luke says, shaking his head.

"One little puff won't hurt you." I light the joint and hold it out to him. He hesitates, then reaches for it.

"You're a bad influence, Kay." He coughs. "It's been a long time."

We finish the joint in silence, taking turns. I'm now pleasantly high. The world seems a happier place, all fuzzy around the edges. I sink back against Luke, against his solid body, and feel his arm go around my shoulder.

"I had nearly stopped, you know," he says lazily.

"Stopped?"

"Shifting. I'd been in the same reality for months. I'd almost forgotten about shifting or what it meant."

"But why?"

"My father had a theory," Luke says.

"Your father? He was a shifter? Is that why you know so much about it?" My words come out in a rush.

Luke shakes his head. "We never talked about it. Wait here. I have something to show you."

He gets up and heads for the bedroom. I notice that he's not walking in an entirely straight line. He returns, holding a leather-bound journal.

I barely have time to register the writing, more printed than written. Precise, in black ink.

Luke reads:

It's been six months since my last shift. I'm winding down, like an old clock that loses minutes by the day. And I'm forgetting.

Marie thinks it's a boy. She's five months, just starting to show. I put my hand on her stomach last night and felt him kick. It made everything so real.

My life has been so unreal, up to now. Shifting. From one world to the next. Started the first time Marie got pregnant. Couldn't handle it. Who could? Only eighteen. After I left, she lost the baby. In all the worlds I visited, she lost the baby.

The guilt gets pretty bad at times.

But, I think it'll work out. Not shifting anymore. It's like a car, see? Purrs like a kitten when you first buy it. But later, stick shift gets all sloppy. Clutch burns out. Hoses need replacing. Transmission goes. One day, the car simply won't turn over.

That's what I think is happening to the old shifting machinery in my head. Won't turn over no more. See, a man's only got so many lives he can lead, so many choices he can make, and then he's stuck with it.

What better place to be stuck? With Marie and the kid.

I promise to do right by them. For once.

I feel like the room chilled down ten degrees. Like a ghost brushed against me.

"Luke, where did you find this?"

"Safe deposit box. After my parents died."

"Any other entries?"

"Only one. Written three years earlier. He lists things, things you might get confused about from shift to shift. Place of work, his best friend's name, Mom's favorite perfume. Nothing important."

I reach for the journal, but Luke closes it. He bites his lip and looks away.

I try to understand. It's all he has left of his father. Maybe he's not quite ready to share that. Maybe he's just a private person. But it hurts, the way he shuts me out.

Hiding my disappointment, I ask, "What do you think happened next?"

"I think he forgot. His clock ran down. The car wouldn't turn over."

"And you?" I manage to say.

"Like I said before, I'd nearly stopped shifting altogether. Meeting you kind of boosted my battery," he says. "Won't last, though. Only so many lives you can lead before you get stuck."

I take a big gulp of wine. "I can't get through this without you."

"Don't worry," he says. "I don't plan to lose you."

He looks at me with such intensity that I believe him. He meets my eyes straight on, not glancing between them or staring at my nose.

"I love the way you do that," I say.

"Do what?"

"Look at me. It's like you don't even notice my eyes."

"They were the first thing I noticed about you," he says. "Your eyes. They're beautiful."

"I'd hardly call them beautiful," I say. "Odd, maybe. Interesting. But most people look away. You don't."

He gets a funny look on his face. "Kay, what's unusual about your eyes?"

Is he *kidding*?

"Well, duh. Nothing except that one is green and the other is brown."

He throws back his head and laughs. I'm getting

annoyed when he says, "I'm a little color blind. I have trouble making out the difference between green and brown."

"So, my eyes look normal to you?"

"Pretty much," he says.

I'm speechless.

Luke finishes his glass of wine, checks his watch. "It's late. I'll take you home."

I smile up at him. "You're trashed, baby. You ain't taking nobody nowhere, nohow."

"You're right," he says with a sheepish smile. "I'll call a cab."

"It's okay. I told my parents I was sleeping over at Sunny's."

"No, it's not okay. Not by a long shot," he says, his smile gone.

"Why not? If you say I'm too young, I'll slug you."

"You're too young," he says.

I pull back my arm to hit him. He blocks me easily. He reaches out to tickle me. Giggling, I fall back on the couch. He keeps tickling, so I fight back, running my fingers along his ribs. He howls with laughter, collapses on top of me.

Everything changes in that moment. His lips are inches away from mine. We stop laughing. My breathing speeds up. My heart is about to burst. I close my eyes, knowing that in the next few seconds he will kiss me. But he doesn't.

"This is all wrong," he says in a hoarse whisper. He gets up. I feel like crying. Or throwing something at him. I pull my legs up under me on the couch and wrap my arms around them. He sits on the other end of the couch, chews on a nail.

"What are you so afraid of?" I demand.

"For one thing, you aren't even legal," he says.

"I'll be eighteen in a month." Actually, it's three months, but I'm not about to tell him that.

He pours more wine, paces back and forth across the tiny living room. "You don't know me. If you knew the truth about the things I've done . . ." He lets the sentence hang in the air.

"Things? What things? Worse than getting high and driving? Knocking down a mailbox and damaging your friend's car?"

"Yeah. Way worse."

"Like what?" I push. "I can't believe you'd ever do anything wrong."

"Yeah, well, shows what you know," he says. "I'll call that cab for you."

He pulls his phone out of his pocket, but I take it out of his hand and place it on the coffee table. I put my arms around his neck and kiss him. It's just a brush of my lips on his. I don't expect him to kiss back. I figure he'll push me away.

Wrong. His hands are warm on my back as he pulls me closer. His lips are on mine. I nearly panic. I don't know how to do this. He'll see that. He'll think I'm a child. But I follow his lead and it's okay. It's more than okay. I get lost in the kiss. I feel light-headed, like I might faint.

He pulls away.

"But I love you."

Wrong. He's suddenly on the other side of the room.

"Where do you see this ending?" he asks me.

I glance down the hallway, toward the bedroom.

"No. Not a chance. We do that and you will hate me. I guarantee it, Kay."

He pours more wine, downs it in one long gulp.

My eyes fill with tears. I've just offered him, well, everything, and he's pushed me aside.

He swears in a barely audible tone. "Okay, look. You can stay the night. You take the bed. I'll take the couch."

"No," I say in a small voice. "I'll be fine on the couch."

He brings me a pillow and some blankets. He heads off to the bedroom, the wine bottle in one hand and his glass in the other.

I try to sleep, I do. But the light comes in from the window. There's a doughnut shop across the street. It's open all night. I hear cars pulling in. Driving away.

I tiptoe down the hall into his bedroom.

"Are you asleep?" I ask.

"No."

I find the bed and crawl in.

"I'll take the couch," he says.

"No. Stay. I'm cold."

"I'll get another blanket."

"I don't want another blanket. I want you." I move next to him so our bodies touch. He's not wearing much, just boxers. I've stripped down to a T-shirt and underwear. He's warm all over.

"Kay . . ." he says in a warning voice.

"Look, I get it," I say.

He's very still. Hardly breathing. "Okay."

"Can I at least lie on your shoulder?" I ask.

Another long pause. "Yes."

He lifts his arm and I slip in. I'm lying on his chest, his arm heavy and warm around me.

I fall asleep to the sound of his heart beating.

Gone

I awake to the sound of snoring. Trojan, I think, reaching out to shake him. I touch bare flesh instead of fur. I roll over to see Luke, mouth open, breathing heavily in my ear.

Memory floods back.

I reach out and stroke his hair, his soft thick black hair. "Wake up, sleepyhead."

"Hmmm?" He stirs, stretches, opens his eyes. I wait for the smile, that sweet, sweet smile.

He looks at me with a blank expression.

"Oh, man." He sits up, pulls the covers around him. "Uh, don't take this the wrong way, but, uh, who are you?"

Betrayal

Who are you?

I'm stunned. I can't speak. He's gone. Shifted. He'd warned me.

You can't remember what happened when the other person was in control.

"Please tell me you aren't as young as you look," he says.

"I'm twenty-one," I say, finding my voice.

"And I met you . . . ?" He gets a vague look on his face.

He doesn't remember me. Every time I've been with him, he's been controlled by Luke's consciousness. *It's like being possessed.* What should I tell him? The truth? I can't. So I lie.

"Last night. Jay's Place. I came in for a drink at the bar. We started talking and I came back here. We shared some wine and . . ."

His eyes dart to the wine bottle, now empty. "How much did I drink?"

"I had two glasses."

"And I drank the rest? Well, that explains the headache." He looks at the bed, then at me. "Ummm . . . did we, uh . . . ?"

"No."

"I'm sorry. I guess I passed out first, huh?" he says, a pained expression on his face.

"Yeah. I guess."

He grimaces. "I don't drink often. For obvious reasons."

I don't know what to say to that. We stare at each other, at a loss for words.

"Ummm," he says, "I have to, uh . . ." He heads to the bathroom, wearing only his boxers.

I'm dressed and ready to go by the time he comes out. He's dressed in jeans and a brown shirt. He looks so good, even hung over, it makes my breath catch.

"Would you like to stay for breakfast?" he offers.

"No, thank you. Maybe you could call me a cab."

"I'm sorry," he says. "When I drink, I kind of black out. Uhh . . . this is really awkward, but I honestly don't remember your name."

"Kay."

He juts out a hand for me to shake. "Pleased to meet you, Kay. I'm Michael."

"What?"

"Michael. Michael Agius."

I shake his hand. I'm numb.
As numb as the night Nick died.

The Same Mistake Twice

I can't get through this. I can't.

I'm in the cab going home. It smells like vinyl seats and pine air freshener. The cabbie has an all-talk radio show on, playing almost inaudibly in the front seat.

How did this happen? How could I have been so stupid? So naive?

So damn young?

He'd lied to me. About the most basic things. His name. His identity.

Why? Did he think I'd never find out? Did he think I was that stupid?

I should have known. I should have. Michael Agius. The driver of the van. Oh, *shit*. Probably the Jay's Place van. The one I'd been riding around in. No, no, the van smelled and looked new.

Of course it did. He probably totaled the van when he hit Nick. When he *killed* Nick.

How dare he come to my brother's funeral? How dare he pretend to be a friend? He'd pursued me from the beginning. Following me, offering me rides, giving me his number. How sick was that? What was he trying to prove? That he could pull one over on me? Kill some guy; date his sister?

And me. Stupid me. Telling him I loved him. He must have laughed at that one. And that whole honorable, hands-off chivalry act. Who was he fooling?

We do that and you will hate me, he'd said. Well, duh. Ya think?

He should have just screwed me and gotten it over with.

I'm sitting on my bed, staring at my phone. I need to talk, but I don't know who to call.

Sunny? Right. Like our last conversation went *so* well. She hasn't spoken to me since. She's still pissed about taking the rap for the accident.

Maya? Maya is so innocent, no fault of her own. How could she possibly understand?

Steph? I've never been close to her. She's a friend through association, through Jen.

Jen? She didn't even come to Nick's funeral.

Who else is there?

Luke? Right. That's Kathleen talking. Kathleen's a suck. Wanting to seek comfort in the very arms of the person who betrayed her. Besides, Luke is gone. Only Michael remains.

So, that leaves Jen. If she'll even speak to me. We haven't talked since the day I turned her away from my door.

I punch in her number. She doesn't answer. I text message her. *Call me. Please.*

In my mind's eye, I imagine her reading the message. Hesitating, finger hovering over the phone. Wondering, *why now?*

My phone rings.

"Jen?" My voice breaks.

"You must have meant to message Sunny," she says in a brittle tone.

"I've done something terrible, Jen."

There is a long pause. I'm about to hang up when she says, "I'll be right there."

I'm sitting on the couch, watching for her car. I open the door as she pulls into the drive.

"Tell me," she says.

But my throat closes up. I can't speak.

Jen makes tea. She knows my house so well she doesn't ask "where's this" and "where's that." She brings two steaming mugs to my bedroom, along with a box of cookies.

"Where'd you find those?" I ask.

"Very back of the pantry," she says. "What's going on here, Kath? Your mom is acting so weird."

"Drunk," I say. "Welcome to Kay's world."

"Kay's world?" Jen's expression is one of concern. "Kath, what's happening? What did you mean on the phone by 'I've done something terrible'?"

"I spent the night with him, Jen."

"With who?"

"The guy who killed Nick. Luke. Only he isn't Luke, he's Michael. He's been lying to me all along."

"Kath, maybe you should back up a bit," Jen says. Her fingers work nervously, plaiting her hair into a braid, then pulling it loose.

"Yeah. I keep forgetting. You're in a different universe."

"Uh, okay. That's one way of putting it," she says, not understanding.

I fill her in: how Luke came to the funeral, how we became friends, how betrayed I felt when I found out his real name was Michael. I leave out the things she wouldn't understand: about shifting, about how Michael had no memory of the things Luke did while possessing him.

Jen forgets to braid her hair when I get to the point where I took the wine and the weed to Luke's apartment. Her eyes go wide in disbelief when I tell her I spent the night in his bed.

"But nothing happened?" she asks.

"He said I'd never forgive him if we did it," I reply. "Well, he got that right. Only why did he start anything in the first place? Why did he come to the funeral? To survey the damage he'd caused?"

"Maybe he came to pay his respects, like every-one else," Jen says.

I'm about to argue that Jen was the one who called Luke a stalker and told me to forget about him. But that was the other Jen, in another reality.

"No. That's just wrong, Jen," I say. "He wasn't family. He wasn't a friend. He had no right to be there."

But even as I say the words, I wonder if they're true. Hadn't Luke said he used to meet Nick for coffee? Is that why he came? And then, once he'd met me, he'd wanted to help me.

No, that's Kathleen talking. Kathleen's a wimp. She'll forgive anyone, for anything. No wonder people take advantage of her. No wonder she fell for Luke.

"Don't you see how wrong it is?" I go on. "How twisted? Did I mention his age? Twenty-three. How sick is that? What does a twenty-three-year-old guy want with a seventeen-year-old girl?"

"You're almost eighteen," Jen reminds me.

"So?" I can't believe her. She was the one who said that it was creepy for a guy that old to be interested in me. Well, the other Jen said it, that is.

"It's not that creepy. I mean, my parents are seven years apart." Jen pulls apart a cookie, licks the white cream filling. "Maybe he really liked you, Kath. Maybe he met you at the funeral and was attracted to you. I mean, what was he supposed to do? Introduce himself as the guy who ran over your brother?"

That pisses me off. "Why are you taking his side?"

Jen dunks the chocolate wafer part into her tea. "I don't know, Kath. It's just sometimes you can be kind of unforgiving, you know?"

"What do you mean?"

"Well, like after the party, when I came over. You wouldn't even talk to me. You wouldn't even let me in the house," she says.

"Me unforgiving? Jen, you could have tried to understand how I felt. But, oh no, not you. You didn't even come to the funeral."

"How could I come?" she says. "You weren't talking to me. Do you think I was going to come, just so that you could snub me again?"

"You *are* one for holding grudges, aren't you?"

"What? Me?" Her voice rises in pitch. "Me, hold grudges? What about you? You blamed me, didn't you? Because you had to call Nick. It was all my fault, wasn't it?"

"If the shoe fits."

Jen's face goes hard. "It was a mistake to come."

"No one is keeping you," I reply.

She sets down her tea. I listen as she walks down the hall, opens and shuts the door. I go into the living room, watch through the window as she walks down my driveway, head held high.

With an awful clarity, I see the split. If I let her go, she will never talk to me again. Will never answer my calls. Will ignore my messages.

I'm about to make the same mistake. Twice. I haven't learned a thing.

I run to the door, dash outside, race down the

driveway. I'm in socks, splashing through slushy snow, slipping, sliding.

"Wait!" I yell.

She turns around. I reach her, throw my arms around her.

I plan to say, "I forgive you."

But at the last second, I change my mind.

"Forgive me?" I beg.

Stuck

I've been Kay for an entire week now. In Hellworld. With a drunk mother and a father who hates me.

There's no sign of Luke. Maybe that's for the best. I can't forgive him for causing my brother's death. Or for lying to me. Or for letting me fall in love with him.

Maybe Jen is right. I'm not a forgiving person. Or maybe some things can't be forgiven.

Sunny hasn't forgiven me. You'd think I was diseased, the way she avoids me. I can't blame her. Kay was a bitch, letting Sunny take the rap for her.

You are Kay, Luke would say.

Yeah, well, I'm sick of being Kay. She's made a mess of everything. I just want to escape.

Maybe you don't, says some part of me, probably Kathleen. Maybe you like being Kay. A little wild; a little uncontrollable. You liked getting Luke drunk. Enjoyed smoking up with him. You liked sleeping in his bed. You threw yourself at him, and it was only his self-control that stopped you.

And why? Because it didn't matter. Because you could shift out. And now you are stuck.

Shut up. *Just shut up.*

But maybe there's a shred of truth in that. I don't admire Kay, but I *like* being her. I *like* saying what I think, doing what I like, going after what I want. Kathleen let people decide for her. Nobody decides for Kay.

So maybe part of me wants to be here, to be Kay. But, let's face it. Kay's life sucks. What if I get stuck here? If I can't shift out? Do I really want to be Kay forever?

Reconciliation

"Sunny, I need to talk to you." I sit down across from her at the lunch table.

"So? Talk."

Those are the first words she's spoken to me in ages. I figure it's an improvement. I push on.

"I'm sorry about . . . I mean, I feel badly that . . ." I groan. This is harder than I thought.

"That night," I say, "that we smoked up and I drove your car. It was my fault, not yours. I was the one who said I should learn to drive."

"So?"

"Look, just take the money for the mailbox, okay? I'm dying of guilt here."

She takes the envelope. She runs a finger along her eyebrow rings.

"You don't have to do this," she says.

"Hell, yeah, I do. I was driving, remember? I knocked it over," I say. "It's the least I can do."

"Thanks," she says, in a muffled tone.

"I'm going to court with you," I say.

"I was the one charged," she says.

Is she protecting me? Still? I suddenly realize that's what she's been doing all along.

"I was the one responsible," I say.

"I got you high."

"Right. How'd you do that, exactly? Tie me up and stick a joint in my face?"

Sunny shifts from foot to foot, fingers her eyebrow rings, touches the studs along her ear. "Ah, hell," she says. She launches herself at me, grabs me with both arms, and hugs the breath out of me.

Rock Climbing

I'm waiting for Dad to get home. As soon as he walks in the door, I say, "We need to talk."

I've already warned Mom that we're having a family conference. She's been nursing a martini for, oh, like the last two minutes. She toddles to the kitchen, mixes another, then sits back down on the living room couch.

"Well?" Dad joins Mom on the couch, and I take the recliner. Only I'm not reclining. I'm perched on the edge of the seat, ready to take off. That's Kate. She hates confrontation, believes the better part of wisdom is avoidance.

"I know I've disappointed you." My hand goes involuntarily to my spiked hair.

"Oh, no, dear," Mom starts to say, but Dad says, "Let her talk."

"I didn't cut and dye my hair to hurt you, Mom. Or do this." I pull up my T-shirt to show her my belly ring.

"Oh, *goodness*." She takes a hasty gulp of martini.

"Kathleen!" Dad says. "Whatever possessed you?"

If he only knew.

But what I say is, "Nothing possessed me, Dad. I just wanted to, I don't know, to exercise some control. Control over myself, over my own body. Is that so bad?"

"By getting a belly ring?"

"It's very pretty. Look." I show Mom, figuring she's a better ally than Dad.

"Did it hurt?" she asks.

"A little." I don't tell her that I wasn't *there* for it, that I popped into Kay's body after the fact.

Dad sighs. "You've changed, Kathleen. Always out with that friend of yours. What's her name?"

"Sunny," Mom volunteers. That surprises me. Maybe she *has* paid some attention to my life.

"Sunny's a good person," I tell them. "I've got a confession to make. I got her in trouble."

"And that would be?" asks Dad.

"She let me drive her car a week or so ago. It was snowing. I swerved to avoid a dog. I spun out and knocked down someone's mailbox."

"Oh, Kathleen," Dad says, "I thought you had more sense than that."

That sets me off. I'm trying to be repentant and all, but now I'm pissed.

"Look, I'm not Nick-the-Wonder-Boy, okay? I'm your stupid, ordinary, screwed-up daughter." I get up. I'm out of there.

"Kathleen!" orders my father. "*Sit.*"

I sit, but I refuse to look at him.

His voice softens, but not much. "What makes you think you mean less to us than Nick did?"

I'm stunned. How could he not know?

"You and Nick? Throwing footballs around in the yard every weekend? Season tickets? Hockey games in winter, soccer, basketball? Dad, was there a weekend you didn't spend with him?"

His face falls. He looks stricken. He looks old.

"Kathleen, when did you show an interest? We asked you, repeatedly, to come with us. You wouldn't come," he says.

Oh, and that is *so* unfair. I hate sports. Hate the whole team thing. Couldn't they have met me half-way? Gone to a movie with me? Taken me out for ice cream? But how can I say that to my father?

And then I think, how can I *not* say it? What do I have to lose at this point?

"Dad, no offense, but I hate team sports. I don't understand the whole testosterone thing. I don't get the rules. But you could have included me, just once. Maybe go out for ice cream. Go to a movie. I don't know. Maybe check out the rock climbing wall at the Y."

"Rock climbing?"

"Yeah. Rock climbing. Maybe lifting weights. Inside stuff, you know? I'm not so much into the elements, okay?"

"Well, sure, we could do that," Dad says. "Sure. That would be good. Rock climbing."

It's the only thing he's heard. But it's a start. Rock climbing. I'm basking in that. It's like a memory of something that hasn't happened yet.

Then Mom brings me back.

"About that accident?" she asks. "Why did you want to drive?"

"Don't you see? If I knew how to drive, Nick would still be here."

"It was an accident," Dad says. "He was on his way to pick you up from a party and—"

"Dad, I went to the party with Jen. She got drunk. I was sober. I could have driven home, if I knew how. I called Nick instead. That's why he's not here. It's my fault. That's why you can't stand to look at me, or talk to me, or—"

Oh, man, I've lost it. I'm crying like a baby now, huge heart-gulping sobs. I feel Dad's arms around me, and I am ten years old again.

Dad says, "It's okay, Kathleen. It was never your fault."

He lets me cry until I'm done, then says, "About learning to drive? Why don't I take you out practice driving again?"

"Remember the last time?"

"Oh. Yeah. Guess I'm not the most patient teacher," Dad says with a wry grin.

"I'll take you," Mom volunteers.

My eyes go to the martini in her hand. She looks at it, then gets up, walks to the kitchen, and pours it down the sink.

"It'll give me a good reason to quit, Kathleen. I should never have started again," she says. "The funny thing is that I never could stand the taste of vodka."

KATHY

Starting Over

I shift during the night. As I shower, I dig into my body's memories. I think I can trace them back to the night that Sunny and I dyed my hair. Only in this reality, I didn't dye my hair. But my mother is still drinking heavily. It's strange, but in a weird way I'm glad. It means dying my hair didn't trigger her descent. She chose that path herself.

Okay, so I didn't dye my hair. I'm not Kate or Kay. But I did go to Sunny's that night. So I'm not Kathleen. I decide to label this Kathy's world. Kathy's branch is where she turned Jen away after the party, went to Sunny's, smoked up, but didn't dye her hair. Seems like Kathy was able to say no. A good sign. I reach further into my memories. I didn't go driving with Sunny, another plus for me.

I also didn't spend the night with Luke. Which

means, theoretically, he could still be here, in this timeline.

My stomach does a flip-flop. Could he be here? Should I call him?

But then I realize my mistake. Luke exists on all timelines, or at least I think he does, but he's not *here*. The part of him that shifts, the part of him I love, the part of him I *hate*, hasn't found his way back to me. If he had, he'd be calling, right now, or knocking on my door.

There is only Michael, and Michael doesn't know me.

It looks like Kathy's world isn't going well. Mom's bedroom door is closed, meaning she is still in bed. Dad's car is gone, meaning he's at work. There's a vodka bottle in the pantry, the level about a third down.

I don't get it. Why did I shift out of Kay's world, just when I'd fixed things up? Or is that the *reason*, however unconscious and random, that I had shifted? My work was done?

I get through the day at school on autopilot, take the bus home. I've made a decision. If I'm stuck here, in Kathy's world, I might as well try to clean up the mess.

Mom is slumped on the couch when I get home. She's got a drink in one hand and a cigarette in the other. When did she add smoking? The house is a disaster—dirty dishes, pizza boxes, empty bottles. And that's just the living room. The kitchen is worse, with weeks' worth of crumbs and food bits on the floor, dishes piled in the sink, an overflowing garbage pail.

It's too much. I'm about to walk away, escape to my room, and lock the door. That's what Kate would do.

Instead, I hunt in the pantry for the vodka bottle. It was a third gone this morning. Now it's down to fumes. I carry it into the living room, set it on the coffee table in front of Mom.

"Tough day?" I ask.

She looks at the bottle. Looks at me. "I only had one or two."

"You drank two thirds of a bottle," I say. "Are you trying to liquefy your liver?"

Mom's face shows her surprise. Then she gets defensive. "I don't have a problem. I can quit anytime."

"Oh, really. How about today?"

"You think I can't do it," she says defiantly.

"No," I say, "I know you can."

Her face crumples as she struggles not to cry. She loses the battle and breaks down into sobs. Embarrassed, I'm about to walk away, to give her some privacy. But that's what I've been doing, in so many worlds. Walking away.

I sit down beside her and put my arm around her. I hold her until she is all cried out.

"I'm a horrible mother," she says. "Ever since Nick died. I haven't taken care of you, or your father, or—"

"Hey," I tell her, "I haven't been much of a daughter, either. Why don't we start over?"

"Starting with this," she says, grabbing her drink. On unsteady legs she walks over to the sink. A few drops of martini splat on the floor, marking her progress, but she doesn't notice. She fishes out the olive, eats it, then pours the martini down the sink.

"I only drink them for the olives," she declares.

That strikes us both as excruciatingly funny.

Shifting

I've been Kathy for several days. After Mom disposed of her hidden vodka stash, we did dishes, cleaned the living room, vacuumed, and dusted. We had dinner ready when Dad came home from work. After I did dishes, I dragged him out of the den, where he'd settled into a sports channel.

"Come on," I said. "I need you to take me practice driving."

His face lit up. "Really? Okay."

He didn't yell once, even when I tried to take off from a stop sign in third gear and stalled the engine. Even when we got home and discovered I'd been driving with the parking brake on the entire time, he didn't yell. Just shook his head and said, "Not bad for a beginner. Not bad at all."

The next day, Friday, Mom made dinner. A real dinner—pot roast and carrots and potatoes and gravy. She made coffee later, to go with cookies and ice cream.

Over dessert, Mom announced her decision to go back to work. Dad said, "That's great! It'll give you something to do."

I checked Kathy's memories. At no time had Dad mentioned Mom's excessive drinking. Maybe Nick masked the fact that my parents never really communicated. Nick talked enough for all of us.

Saturday, Mom and I drove to the mall to buy her new clothes. I made her try on a plum sweater. It looked great, a big change from the browns and grays she usually wears.

And on Sunday, I made up with Jen. I baked a cake with chocolate icing and wrote "I'm Sorry" on it.

She forgave me.

All this time, while I've been fixing Kathy's life, I've been thinking about two people: Nick and Luke.

Nick. My fault that he died. And now it's not just me who pays, it's my parents, our relatives, Nick's friends. Everyone who knew him.

And Luke. How can you love and hate a person, all at the same time? If he showed up tomorrow on my doorstep, I don't know what I'd do: slam the door in his face or jump into his arms. Maybe it's best he hasn't returned. On the other hand, part of me is terrified that I'll never see him again.

I must be the most messed-up person in this universe. What do I see in Luke, anyway? When I said I loved him, I meant it. But what kind of love? Based on *what*?

Attraction? Yes, from the first moment I saw him. Need? Yes, from the first time I cried all over him. Caring? There's no doubt he cared for me. Showed up when I needed him. Rescued me when I screwed up.

So, what was he? A brother substitute? At first.

A father substitute? Maybe a little. My own father barely knew I existed. It wasn't until I reached out to him that things changed. Luke was the one who was there for me, in all the worlds, shifting with me, supporting me.

When did I start falling in love with him? From that first moment, when he wiped away my tears? At the skating rink, when he'd said, "I'm not your father," and looked like he wanted to kiss me?

I love my dog, but I could learn to live without him. Can I live without Luke?

Not that it's my choice, whether I get to live with him or without him. He'd warned me about drinking and losing control. *I worry that one day, if I'm not careful, I'll shift so far away I'll never find my way back to where I want to be.*

And what had I done? Ignored his words, poured glass after glass of wine for him. Threw myself at him. Got him so upset he took the rest of the wine to his room and drank it.

I doubt I will ever see him again. I wouldn't even know how to begin. He could be anywhere. What had he said? An infinity of universes?

I'm sitting in the car, thinking it over. I have the engine turned on, the music blaring. I run through the gears, over and over. I put the car into reverse, go to the end of the driveway, shift into first, and drive back up.

Over and over.

Dad's been out once to check on me. I told him I needed practice shifting.

Shifting. Ha. If only he knew.

One thing keeps going through my mind. That night that I'd gone to bed in Nick's bed and woken up in my own. I had found the toothpaste tube mangled the way Nick always left it. I'd gone back to bed in my own bed, but woke up again in Nick's. The toothpaste tube was now smooth. Had I shifted during the night to a timeline where Nick existed?

So why had I shifted back to my own timeline?

To be with Luke?

ALL OF US

Without Him

I continue to shift, spending a few days in each place, trying my best, succeeding, failing, moving on.

Kay went to Teen Court with Sunny and owned up to the damage to the mailbox. A jury of their peers sentenced them both to community service. So now, she and Sunny are shoveling driveways and cleaning out basements for elderly people. The seniors are so grateful that they ply the girls with hot chocolate and homemade cookies. Kay thinks that after she serves her sentence, she might sign up as a volunteer with Helping Hands for Seniors. Her only worry is that she might get fat.

Other timelines aren't so great. In some, Mom is still drinking. In a few, she's so heavy into her MADD meetings that she's never home. In those realities, Dad either watches sports or plays online games.

The timelines fracture, splitting again and again. I move through many different realities, many universes.

All of them without Luke.

KATHLEEN

Found and Lost

It's Friday night. Mom and Dad have gone over to Aunt Lydia's for the evening. I'm in the living room, watching a movie, eating corn chips with nacho cheese dip.

The doorbell rings. I peer out the window to see a stocky figure in a suede jacket.

"Kathleen!" Luke's face is radiant with joy. He steps forward, arms outreached.

I'm Kathleen. Kathleen does not stand up for herself. She doesn't. Only, I am no longer just Kathleen. I'm the sum of all of my selves. I hesitate. I don't know how to react. Jump into his arms? Tell him all is forgiven? Or will I slam the door in his face?

"Hello, *Michael*," I say.

Well, at least now I know how I will react.

He shuts his eyes and swears under his breath.

Then he looks at me and says, "Kathleen. I can explain."

"Not interested." That's Kay talking. She likes to be in control.

"Please, hear me out. I've gone through a hundred universes to find you again. You can't turn me away."

"Watch me." I start to close the door. But I don't know what I'll do if he walks away. None of us know what we will do if he walks away.

He catches the door with his hand, holds it open. Cold air flows past me; flows into me.

"Didn't it mean anything to you?" he asks.

"No." Kay again. She lies.

"It meant everything to me," he says.

"What part, Luke? Or should I say *Michael*?"

His face hardens. I've pushed too hard.

Then his expression changes. He chews on a nail, frowning, then drops his arms by his sides.

"It doesn't matter if you believe me or not," he says. "I love you."

Kate snorts inside my head. I tell her to shut up. I'm in charge now. I blink back tears. I want to believe him, I do.

"Please," says Luke, "may I come in?"

I glance behind me at the house where my brother once lived.

"No," I say.

"My place then. Come with me?"

The pleading in his eyes melts the ice in me. "I'll get my coat."

The silence in the car is strained. When we arrive, I go to the bathroom and run cold water over my face. I come out to find coffee, hot and strong, and cake, topped with brown sugar and nuts and cinnamon.

I could hate Luke more easily if he wasn't such a good cook.

I drink my coffee, eat a piece of cake, and wait. He leans forward, rests his arms on his elbows, clasps and unclasps his hands. Wide hands; competent hands. I want to trust him, I do.

"I left work about one in the morning. New Year's Eve." He stops to rub his eyes. "I've asked myself, if I hadn't been so tired, would it have happened? Would I have reacted quicker?"

I'm listening, but Kay thinks he's making a bid for her sympathy. I tell her and the others to keep their opinions to themselves. I'm in control now.

"I swear, Kathleen, the police report was right. I was stone-cold sober. You know that. I don't drink." He clears his throat. "Not often, anyway."

I'm still listening, even through my anger.

"Was I going too fast for the conditions? I've asked myself that. It's the worst feeling. Knowing it's going to happen. Feeling powerless to prevent it." He stops. Reaches for his coffee. Gulps it.

"When were you going to tell me?" I ask.

He looks down at his hands. "I don't know."

"You had no right to show up at the funeral home," I say.

"I *know*. I just wanted to say I was sorry. To someone. Anyone."

"So the guilt would go away?"

"It will never go away, Kathleen." He rubs the palms of his hands together, then stares at them. I should feel sympathy for him, but I don't.

"Why did you give me your number? Hadn't you done enough damage?"

He flinches. "It was wrong. I know that. I just felt awful. I wanted to make up for it at first. Later, I started falling for you."

"So you built our relationship on a lie."

"I built it on many lies." He's looking down at his hands, speaking so softly I can barely hear the words.

Many lies?

"Go on," I say, through clenched teeth.

"I wasn't a student at the college. They don't even teach culinary arts."

"*What?* Why?"

"I couldn't tell you the truth. That I was responsible for—" He takes another gulp of coffee. "So, I made up a story about meeting your brother. About having coffee with him. I needed some reason why I came to the funeral home." He rubs his palms again.

"It all makes sense now," I say. "You telling me that Nick's death was no one's fault. It was an accident, you said."

He buries his face in his hands.

"And you were so evasive, about everything. Your past. The mistakes you had made. Your father's journal."

"His last name was in it. Agius. I was afraid you would recognize it," Luke says, looking up. His face is streaked with tears. "You must hate me."

"Maybe I should," I say, after thinking it over. "But I can't."

He nods, accepting that for what it is.

"There's more," he says.

"I'm waiting."

"When you shift, and I follow you, it doesn't just *happen*. You don't just pull me along." He takes a quick glance at me, then looks away. "The first time, I had your pen in my pocket. I didn't deliberately take it. I absentmindedly stuck it there. I came home and lay down on the couch, too exhausted to take off my coat. I fell asleep. And in the morning, I figured I'd shifted."

"How did you know?"

"I looked at myself in the mirror," he says.

I nod, remembering the times I'd looked at my reflection and saw a phase-shifted face, like a double exposure or like looking through bad 3-D glasses.

"It was odd," he says, "because I'd pretty much stopped shifting at that point. So, I went back to the funeral home—"

"I thought I saw you—"

"And there you were, on the second night of the visitation. You looked out of focus. Phase-shifted, as you call it. I knew then that I'd shifted onto a branch caused by a split in your timeline."

"Yes, the first split. When I turned Jen away in one reality, and made up with her in another."

He nods.

"Why would having my pen . . . ?" I start to say.

And then I get it.

"Oh, something I had touched. Fingerprints, oils from my hand. Sweat."

"Yes. Part of you, still there on the pen. I also had the handkerchief."

"My tears."

"Yes. In each new world I needed something of yours, in order to follow you when you shifted again."

"The rose. Jen saw you take a rose off the casket."

"It was the rose you had placed there. And it was me that night going through your recycling bin. Finding your water bottle."

"Wait," I say. "How did you know where I lived?"

He glances up. "You're in the phone book."

Duh, thinks Kate. I tell her to shut up.

"How could you tell it was my water bottle?" I ask. "Not my mom's or dad's?"

"Don't know. It just felt *different* from the other bottles. I can't explain it."

"But, wait. I don't get it. Why lie to me? Why not just tell me you needed something of mine to follow me?"

Luke slowly meets my eyes. He looks beaten. He looks lost.

And then I finally understand. By having something of mine, he could follow me between universes. And if I had known that all I needed was something of my brother's . . .

"Luke, how *could* you?" I say. Well, not quite say it. It's more like I scream it.

His eyes drop.

"All these months, I could have been with Nick," I shout.

"And without me," he whispers.

I pick up my coffee. It's cold. I drink it, just the same, buying time. My feelings are so mixed up, I don't know *what* to feel.

"What do you mean, *without you*?" I say, once I think I can control my voice. "You could follow me. I find Nick, and you find me."

He shakes his head. "Only so many shifts a person can make, Kathleen. I'm done. It's a miracle I made it back this one last time."

"So it's all my fault? Making you lose control? Causing you to shift randomly?" I know I'm being irrational, but I can't help it.

"No," Luke says, with an edge to his voice. "I didn't say it was your fault. I was stupid, that's all. I should have known better."

That stings, the anger in his voice. Then I realize he's angry at himself, not me.

"So how did you find me this time?" I ask, striving for calmness.

"Pure chance. I shifted into a world that we'd both been in. The one with the rose. It brought me back to you."

"So, I'll give you something of mine," I say. "Here, my school ring."

He takes the ring and slips it onto his baby finger, but I can tell by his expression that he's given up.

"Look," he says. "I don't even think it's *possible* for you to find your brother. You've been making little shifts between adjacent branches of the tree. You're talking about a jump across a life-changing event, over to a completely different timeline, on the opposite side of the tree."

"How do you know it's not possible? Did you ever try?"

He sounds tired as he says, "When my parents died. When your brother died. Yes. I've tried. I've *never* jumped that far. I can't."

He's killing me. I don't want to cry, I *won't* cry, but I do. He pulls a hankie out of his pocket and offers it to me. I blot my eyes with it, and, after a moment's hesitation, blow my nose.

And then it dawns on me. My heart races and I feel like there's not enough oxygen in the room.

"But I can," I say. "I can, because I *have*."

"What do you mean?"

"This one night, I missed Nick so much. And I was so angry. Angry at him for leaving. Angry at his girlfriend, Nadia, for getting so close to my mom. I smashed a photo, one of Nadia and Nick, on the bathroom floor."

I check Luke's expression. It's worry.

"After I smashed the picture, I put on an old shirt of Nick's. I slept on top of his bed, holding his old teddy bear."

"You shifted?" Luke asks. "You shifted to a universe where he existed?"

"I think so," I say. "There was this toothpaste tube—"

"Toothpaste tube?"

"Yes. We shared a bathroom. Nick always scrunched up the toothpaste. Drove me crazy. After he died, I'd smoothed out the tube. The way I like it. But that night, I woke up. The smashed photo was gone. The toothpaste tube was scrunched in the middle."

"You're basing a lot on toothpaste and broken glass," Luke says.

"No. He was alive. I know it."

"You didn't see him," Luke argues. "You have no way of knowing."

"Sometimes you have to believe," I say.

Luke's shaking. He picks up his coffee mug, stares at it. I know, without knowing how I know, that he is thinking about heaving it across the room.

He sets it down. Gently.

Our universe just split again.

"You're going to leave me, aren't you?" Luke asks. "You're going to find him."

"I have to," I say. "I couldn't live with myself if I didn't try."

"I can't follow you. I've lied about a lot of things. Not this one."

"I *have* to do this," I say.

"You told me you loved me."

"I meant it. I still do." I take a deep breath. "But I love my brother, too."

It doesn't seem enough, but I don't know what else to tell him.

"When?" he asks.

"Tonight."

"No," he says. "Give *me* tonight."

I call home. No one answers, so I leave a message on the machine, saying I'm staying over at Jen's house.

Nothing happens; everything happens. We talk and we talk. And that's it, but it's more than enough.

I finally fall asleep, cocooned in his arms.

In the morning, I wake up to find him sitting on the edge of the bed.

"Did you sleep at all?"

He shakes his head.

"You'll find me," I insist.

He struggles to keep his composure.

I call a cab.

He doesn't look up when I leave.

Decision

He'll find me. I know he will. He has to.

What am I doing? My brother exists in another timeline, another branch of the tree. Isn't that enough for me? Why do I need to be there with him? Why do I need to find him? I'll see him through different eyes. He won't be the god he used to be. He'll be human, and his feet will stink enough to clear the room when he takes off his shoes.

But family is everything, right? If my brother is still alive, I have to find him.

Don't I?

All day Sunday, I struggle with myself. If my plan

works, I'll see Nick in the morning. It will be as if I'd never made the wrong decision about the party. As if it never happened.

But I know that isn't true. It did happen. And in all those universes created by that fatal split, Nick is gone forever, leaving myself, Nadia, and my parents to cope with our grief.

Don't be an idiot, Kay tells me. You've done everything you can for those people, in each universe. You changed their lives for the better, or at least you tried. Go home.

And me, as Kathleen, doesn't want to leave my parents behind, alone, without Nick, without me. But that's ridiculous. I'll still be here, Kathleen will. It's only my self-awareness that shifts. My parents will never feel the loss.

But I will.

I start to dial Luke's number a dozen times, but I don't complete the call. What could I possibly say to him that I haven't already said?

In the end I say goodnight to my parents, give them both a hug, and get ready for bed.

Mom and Nadia have cleaned out Nick's room in this timeline, but I have several things of his—the football jersey, his teddy bear, his mug with jugs. Hopefully, traces of Nick remain. I wear the jersey, and climb into bed with the teddy bear and the mug.

It takes me a very long time to fall asleep.

Home

I am awake. I lie in bed, eyes closed. Did I do it? Have I shifted?

I hear the toilet flush.

My legs don't want to hold my weight. I stumble to the bathroom, open the door, stare at the counter beside the sink.

There's a tube of toothpaste, scrunched in the middle.

I fling open the door to Nick's room.

"Hey! Ever hear of knocking?" Nick is getting dressed, pulling on his boxers. He dives into bed and yanks up the covers.

"Hi," I say in a voice that doesn't quite work.

"Hi, yourself," he says. "Mind giving me some privacy?"

I back out, into our shared bathroom, and close his door. I lock it so he can't come in. I turn on the shower so he won't hear me. I'm torn between laughing and crying.

I do both.

Tradeoff

Nadia comes over midafternoon. We play Monopoly. Nick cheats. He wins. At five, he and Nadia leave for dinner.

"Where are you going?" I ask.

"Same as usual," Nick answers. "Jay's Place."

Jay's Place. That's their *usual*? It hits so hard that I have to catch my breath. I wonder, is Luke working tonight? Will he cook their dinner?

I want to go with them. Run into the kitchen, grab Luke, and say, "I made it! I did it!"

But he wouldn't know me. He'd be the Luke, no, *correction*, Michael, on the timeline where we never met. On the other huge branch of the tree where I didn't go to the party with Jen, didn't call Nick for a ride home.

I have dinner with my parents, then go over to Jen's for a sleepover. We fill Maya in on the latest reality shows. We talk about boys. We eat pizza and drink soda and play board games. I wake up in the morning and I am where I should be. At Jen's, in her family room, in my sleeping bag.

At noon, Jen drives me home. My day is normal. I do homework, listen to music, catch up on e-mails. Nick works on his car in the garage, changing his oil and replacing his brake pads. I go in and watch, not because I'm interested in cars but because I can't look at him enough.

I guess it shows. At one point, he wipes his hands on a rag and asks, "You okay?"

"Never been better," I say.

He gives me a big-brother hug. He smells like grease and oil. It's a great smell. It's real and solid, something I can hold on to. Is it enough? I tell myself this is what I wanted.

Maybe if I keep saying it, I will start to believe it.

Fading

I am awake. I remember I used to play some kind of game about being awake, but I can't remember what it was. Something about guessing where I am. Dumb game. I'm in my own bed, where I wake up every morning. Duh. Ya think?

It hits me as I'm getting dressed for school.

I'm forgetting.

My memory is fading, like an old photograph left too long in the sun. The edges curl and the images grow faint. The colors bleed away, leaving indistinct people with blurry faces.

Maybe that's my mind, trying to protect itself. Not for the first time do I wonder if I'm psychotic, if all these lives and timelines are the products of my own insanity. Kathleen, Kay, Kate, Kathy—how could I have been all of them? And all at the same time?

I should write it all down, I should. I grab a spiral notebook with a red cover from my desk. I open it and begin to write.

My memory is fading, like an old photograph left too long in the sun.

Choices

Days turn into weeks, weeks into months. The cold of winter gives way to soft winds and the scent of lilacs in bloom. The warm days of spring give way to the heat of summer. And summer will soon give way to the first cool nights of fall.

Nick and Nadia announce their wedding date, next spring. Trojan gets a little more gray in his muzzle. Mom and Dad get along as they have always gotten along—polite, comfortable, set in their routines, without any real intimacy. I am accepted to the University of Wisconsin–Eau Claire, the same college as Nick and Nadia. I learn to drive; I get my license. For my eighteenth birthday, my parents buy me a used car. It's old, but it will get me back and forth to campus every day. It's only a half-hour drive, over country roads. Even I can handle that.

Everything is as it should be, but I am empty inside. I look at Nick and Nadia and think, *they are soul mates.*

And where is my soul mate? In what universe? Does he still remember me?

Every night, before bed, I read my journal. I remind myself of who I am, who I've been, and whom I've loved. I'm afraid. Have I made the wrong decision? There is no going back. No way to find Luke. I could travel through a million universes and not find him. I need an object, something he touched when he was Luke. I have no such object.

And then it happens. Pure chance.

I'm filling out financial aid forms for school. My pen runs dry. I rifle through the junk drawer in the kitchen, come up with one highlighter and one pencil with a broken lead.

"Are there no pens in this house?" I grumble, to no one in particular.

Nick walks by, wearing his football jacket, on his way to pick up Nadia for a date. He pats his pockets, pulls out a pen, hands it over.

"No need to get excited," he says.

"I hate filling out these stupid forms."

"Yeah, doesn't everyone? Look, fill it out and leave it on the table. I'll look it over for you, make sure you didn't make any mistakes."

"Thanks!"

Nick has one hand on the doorknob when I notice the pen. Jay's Place is written in flowing script, gold lettering on a scarlet background, along with a phone number. My breath sticks in my throat. There's something about this pen. It almost shimmers in my hand.

"Nick? Who gave you this pen?"

"Huh?" He comes back, takes it from me, examines it. "I can't remember."

"*Think!*" My words come out a little sharper than I'd intend.

Nick's dark eyebrows form a frown. "Uh, let's see. Oh, yeah. The chef, the guy at Jay's Place? Nadia really liked his veal Parmesan. Asked him for the recipe. He wrote it down for her. I guess I kept the pen by accident."

"When?" I croak, my throat dry.

"What does it matter?" Nick says, looking at his watch. "Look, I'm late. Can't it wait?"

"No, it can't. Please, Nick."

Nick sighs in resignation. "Okay, okay. Let's see. We stopped for dinner because . . . oh, yeah, I remember. We'd been Christmas shopping and Nadia said she was starving. So we went for dinner. That's it. Nadia had veal. I had steak. Does that help?"

"More than you know," I say.

Christmas shopping. That means it was a few weeks before the accident. Before everything changed. There's a good chance that Luke was in Michael's body. That Luke touched this very pen.

"You're one weird little sister," Nick says, grinning. "Can I go now? Nadia hates to be late for a movie."

"Wait." I throw my arms around him and hug him, hard. Nick bear-hugs me back.

"What's with the sudden show of affection?" he asks.

"I am going to miss you so very much," I say, with tears in my eyes. "I love you."

"Uh, yeah. Well, I love you too, but I'm not moving out all that soon, okay?" He grins, gives me a quick hug, and heads for the door.

I wait until he's gone before I whisper, "But I am."

I say goodnight to my parents. They don't know it means good-bye. To them, it doesn't. I'll still be here in the morning. Still be their daughter. But it won't be *me*. I'm leaving.

I'm dismayed to find I have no special words for them. Just "I love you," which isn't enough. I tell myself I will see them again, very soon, tomorrow morning in fact. But they will be *different* parents, in a different universe.

If all goes well, I will wake up in Luke's reality. Correction: not *his* reality, since there are infinite variations of that, but in the last reality in which we were together.

Will he remember me? Or has his memory faded, like a photograph left too long in the sun?

I crawl into bed, clutching his pen in my hand. Of all the choices I have made, this is the hardest one. I wonder if later I will tell myself I did the right thing.

Eventually, I fall asleep.

A Different Universe

And wake up. It's morning. I play the game. The game I used to play. Can I guess where I am without opening my eyes?

My hair isn't spiked. It's grown out, past my shoulders. I check my navel. No belly ring. I'm wearing pajamas, my Tigger ones. Trojan is asleep on my bed, his head on the pillow beside me. He wakes up, licks my face, goes back to sleep.

In the bathroom, the toothpaste tube is smooth, just the way I like it. I open the door to Nick's room. His belongings are gone.

It hits me again, like the first time, like I've lost him all over again. I remind myself he is still alive, in another universe. I remind myself of why I have done this, again trading one choice for another. I will *not* cry. I won't.

The room is now an office, with a laptop humming away on top of a sleek desk. I glance at the screen. Mom's writing the novel she said she wanted to write.

She comes into the room, carrying a cup of coffee.

"Hi, hon," she says. "You're up early. Everything okay?"

"Yes," I say. "Just meeting a friend for breakfast."

I hope.

I've learned to drive in this timeline as well, though my car is a different make. I drive over to Jay's Place, my stomach in knots. When I arrive, I find a new name on the restaurant. Michael's.

Inside the restaurant, everything is changed. The lobster traps are gone. The lower part of the walls is faced in brick, a deep red-brown. Murals decorate the upper walls—blue sky and ocean, cliffs, snug harbors, dusty stone ruins. All drenched in sunlight.

I remember that Michael's parents came from Malta. I guess this is what it might have looked like.

The tabletops are covered with smooth tiles that match the rougher tiles of the floor. The overall effect is one of warmth and welcome. I order an omelet. It's the same as the first time. Awesome.

Afterward, I ask the waitress if I might speak to the chef.

He walks out of the kitchen, wiping his hands on his apron. His hair is a bit shorter, and he's thinner. I think there might be smudges under his eyes, but with his complexion, and the dim light in the restaurant, it's hard to tell.

"Hi," he says, with absolutely no sign of recognition.

"Hi," I say back. "You do amazing things to an omelet."

"Yeah?" he says, his eyes lighting up. "That's what I always tell people."

"So, when did you start opening for breakfast?"

"Shortly after I bought the place from Jay," he says. "Made sense. Increased business."

I smile.

He smiles.

Conversation dies.

"Do you happen to have any pie?" I ask, trusting my instincts.

"For breakfast? Isn't that a bit decadent?"

Yes. Does he remember?

"I ate my eggs," I say.

He grins, but still shows no sign of recognition. "So you did. What kind of pie would you like?"

"Peach."

He grimaces. "Sorry, I hate peach pie. Never could stomach it."

"Some things are immutable," I say.

"Exactly." He gives me a puzzled look, as if he's searching his memory. His face shifts, just for a second, like a double exposure.

Luke. He's in there, *somewhere.*

"How about apple pie?" I suggest. "And coffee?"

"Sure. That I can do."

"Join me?" I ask.

"I beg your pardon?"

"Take a break. Sit down. Have some pie."

He hesitates. I know what he's thinking. So damn young.

"It's just pie," I tell him.

He flushes. Bites a nail.

"I guess it would be okay," he says with a hesitant

smile. "I ate my eggs this morning, too."

He walks through the swinging door into the kitchen.

I follow.

He shoots me a startled look when I sit down at the little table where he served me apple pie, many months and universes ago.

"I've always liked eating in the kitchen. Less formal," I say by way of explanation. I can't tell him the real reason. I'm hoping that if I can re-create some of our past interactions, it will jar loose a memory.

"You certainly seem to know your own mind," he says. "For someone so, uh . . ."

"Young?" I supply.

He nods, looks uncomfortable.

"I'm eighteen."

"Oh," he says, visibly relaxing. He pours coffee, adds cream to mine, no sugar. He places a slice of Cheddar cheese on top of my pie without asking and hands it to me.

I want to jump up and down. *Yes.* Some part of him remembers.

We eat in silence.

"Another slice?" he offers.

"No thanks, Luke," I say, watching carefully for his reaction.

He just about falls off his chair. "How did you know my middle name?"

"Is it your middle name?"

"Yes. Michael Lucas Agius," he says.

"Hi. I'm Kath," I tell him.

"Nice to meet you, Kath," he says, holding out his hand. He looks at me quizzically for a second, then wraps his other hand around mine. He phase-shifts again, just briefly. "I'm having a déjà vu experience here," he says, his eyes dark, dark but with a glimmer of starlight.

"Maybe we knew each other in a different lifetime," I suggest.

"Or a different universe," he says.

We sit there, not speaking, my hand still in his. The silence draws out, becomes awkward. He lets go of my hand, checks his watch.

"Whoa. Better get busy with dinner prep. You need a ride home?"

"No, thanks," I say. "I have a car."

"Hey, no kidding. When did you learn to drive?"

"This winter," I say.

"That's great," he says. "So what was that story about your dog, anyway?"

"Trojan?"

"Yes. He wasn't really named after—"

"No," I say. "Dad wanted to name him Prince, and Mom said King. And I said he was as big as a horse . . ."

"A Trojan horse?"

"Yeah. My brother thought it was kind of funny."

"Why so sad?" Luke asks. "Did you lose him? Your brother?"

"Life is full of tradeoffs," I say.

He nods but looks puzzled.

I want to do a happy dance. He's dipping into memories he doesn't remember he has. He's still *there.*

He helps me on with my coat, opens the kitchen door for me, walks me through the restaurant. We get to the door, and he puts his hand on the handle but doesn't open it. He reaches out and touches my face.

"You were crying. You were sitting there, on a bench, all alone, crying. I felt awful. Like I had caused your grief," he says.

He shakes his head. "But that's insane. We've just met. I mean we *did* just meet, didn't we? I don't know you, do I?"

"No, not yet," I say. *"But you will."*

Deborah Lynn Jacobs says, "I've always wondered about the road not taken. Let's face it. Life is a series of choices. What if you made different choices? How would your life turn out? We can't see down those other branches in the road. We don't know how things might have turned out if we had made a different choice.

"And what about the little decisions we make every day—they seem unimportant, but are they? Let's say you decide not to take a jacket with you to work. You catch a cold. You get pneumonia, end up in hospital, and fall in love with the cute male nurse who works the night shift. Hey, it could happen!

"I will never know how my life would have turned out had I made different choices along the way. But I do know Kathleen's life, and where her decisions led her. That was the fun part of writing this book."

Deborah Lynn Jacobs's choices have taken her down many roads. Her jobs have included library page, theater usher, lab assistant, cleaning lady, telemarketer, waitress, receptionist, college counselor, college instructor, life skills coach, freelance writer, novelist and mom. She has lived in nine cities, so far, in both Canada and the United States, and now lives in Wisconsin.

About the Author

CHOICES

Y JAC   2/08

Jacobs, Deborah Lynn.

Choices /

DH